CLARE BALDING

The Racehorse Who Learned to Dance

Illustrated by TONY ROSS

PUFFIN

PUFFIN BOOKS

UK | USA | Canada | Ireland | Australia
India | New Zealand | South Africa

Puffin Books is part of the Penguin Random House group of companies
whose addresses can be found at global.penguinrandomhouse.com.

www.penguin.co.uk   www.puffin.co.uk   www.ladybird.co.uk

First published 2019
This edition published 2020

001

Text copyright © Clare Balding, 2019
Illustrations copyright © Tony Ross, 2019

The moral rights of the author and illustrator have been asserted

The lyrics on p. 249 and p. 251 are from 'This Is Me', written by Justin Paul
and Benj Pasek. Those on p. 282 and p. 284 are from 'The Greatest Show',
written by Ryan Lewis, Justin Paul and Benj Pasek. Both songs feature on
The Greatest Showman : Original Motion Picture Soundtrack
(Atlantic Records, December 2017)

Set in 12.25/20 AbsaraOT
Printed in Great Britain by Clays Ltd, Elcograf S.p.A.

A CIP catalogue record for this book is available from the British Library

ISBN: 978-0-241-33676-2

All correspondence to:
Puffin Books
Penguin Random House Children's
80 Strand, London WC2R ORL

*With affection and admiration for those
special horses and ponies who change our lives*

The Folly Farm family

Charlie

Granny Pam

Mr Bass

Mrs Bass

Harry

Larry

Polly

Joe

Chapter 1

'Will it ever rain again, Charlie?' Bill Bass's voice was muffled as he asked the question from beneath Taylor Swift's udder.

'I don't know, Dad. I thought it *always* rained in summer.' Charlie scratched Taylor Swift's nose. The milking machine was attached now and the cow's udder began squirting out warm white liquid.

Charlie sighed. 'The grass has gone brown and I keep worrying that Noddy will get sunstroke, out in the field all day.'

Noddy was their nickname for Noble Warrior, the racehorse they had bought by accident two years ago. Against all the odds and with the help of his best friend, Percy the pony, Noble Warrior had won the Derby – and a million pounds in prize money. Later that summer, he had been kidnapped after an Open Day at the farm, and although Charlie and her brothers had rescued him before any physical harm was done, the experience had left Noddy traumatized. Now he was terrified of carriages, men with long whips, and large crowds, and when he got himself in a panic he was a danger to everyone. Charlie had decided the only answer was to end her beloved horse's racing career and he was now enjoying his retirement by relaxing in the field at Folly Farm.

'I wouldn't worry too much,' said Bill, standing up and moving on to the next cow. 'They're pretty bright, these animals. I've seen Percy and Noddy up at the edge of the wood keeping under the shade of the trees. And as for this lot . . .'

He pointed at the long line of cows.

'They stand in the river all day munching the grass on the banks. Princess Anne and Madonna get the best spots and they only come in when it's milking time. They've been round the block, those two, and they know what's what!' He stroked Madonna's back fondly.

'But what if we run out of grass?' Charlie was seriously worried. She'd seen a feature on the news about farmers whose grass had stopped growing. They'd had to feed the animals hay, and supplies were running low.

'We'll deal with that problem if we have to, my love,' Bill said calmly. 'Don't you be worrying about things we can't control. We'll always do right by our animals! Anyway, we're due a big storm early next week so the boys can stop doing that rain dance of theirs soon.'

He laughed as he moved on to the next cow. As Charlie walked out of the milking shed she could see Harry and Larry lining up the chickens into a formation. Larry started stomping his right foot to the beat of a drum that Harry was pounding. The chickens looked confused and the two at the back tried to shuffle towards the hen house.

Charlie had never understood how her brothers' brains worked. They were occasionally useful and had helped her solve the mystery of who kidnapped Noble Warrior after he had won the Derby, but most of the time they acted like idiots.

'I don't think the chickens want to dance in this *heat*!' Charlie shouted out to her brothers.

Harry and Larry turned to look at her and both nodded their heads as if they agreed. But as they continued to nod, Charlie realized it was all part of the dance – they were stamping and nodding all at the same time. She wasn't sure they'd mastered the finer points of the drum rhythm.

Then Charlie's attention was grabbed by a car pulling into the farmyard. It was the Williams's Range Rover with Mrs Williams at the wheel and Charlie's best friend, Polly, in the passenger seat. Charlie's heart skipped a beat. Polly had been badly injured when Noble Warrior's kidnappers had

driven recklessly past her pony, who had spooked and reared. For a few days, Polly's life had hung in the balance. She made it through but had to have multiple operations before she could move around in a wheelchair. Now, ten months on, she was starting to learn how to walk again, using a crutch to support her. The nerve damage from her fall meant that she had little feeling in her left side and sometimes, when she was sitting, her left leg or arm would jump in jerky, involuntary movements.

Charlie ran to the Range Rover and opened the back door as soon as it pulled up, throwing her arms round her friend before she could even get out.

'Careful now, Charlie,' said Mrs Williams gravely. 'You know we have to be gentle with Polly. She's very fragile.'

Polly made a face as she reached for her crutch, swung her legs out of the car and took a hesitant step forward. Once she had steadied herself, she leaned her crutch against the side of the car so that she could fling her arms back round Charlie in a big hug. She whispered in her ear, 'I'm fed up with people treating me as if I'm made of china. I may be dented, but I'm not broken!'

Charlie smiled at her friend. She remembered how Polly had been the only one able to calm Noble Warrior down after he had been frightened by a carriage on the road outside. There was nothing fragile about her attitude! She was the bravest person Charlie knew.

Polly and Charlie walked slowly across the cobbled farmyard to the back door of the farmhouse.

'I'm sure Mum will want to see you, Mrs Williams. Come in for a cup of tea –' she glanced behind at Polly's mother '– or maybe something cold?'

'Ooh, that would be nice. I'll have a glass of water, please, Charlie!' replied Mrs Williams.

Charlie was in awe of Polly's mother. She was so stylish and graceful. Today she was wearing a pretty patterned dress and, while everyone else looked as if they were melting, Mrs Williams was ice-cool.

Polly was coming to stay for a couple of days. It was the first time since she had come out of hospital that she'd been allowed to spend a night away from home.

'Now, Charlie,' said Mrs Williams. 'I've made a list of the various pills Polly has to take and the exercises she must do this evening and in the morning. I'll talk your mother through it all as well, but I would appreciate it if you made sure she did them! She's been making wonderful progress, but we can't afford to let up now. Can I trust you?'

'Yes, of course you can, Mrs Williams,' Charlie said seriously. 'You know I will do everything I can to support Polly. She's my best friend in the whole world.'

'Ah, Jasmine!' Charlie's mother, Caroline, charged into the room, wiping beads of sweat from her forehead. She left a dark grey smudge of mud on her cheek. 'I'm so sorry I wasn't here to say hello. I've just been feeding the pigs and tidying up the muck heap. Do I smell?'

Mrs Williams wrinkled her nose and said kindly, 'Oh, not too badly. I suspect they'd bottle it up in

America and sell it as *Eau de Farmyard*. You could make a fortune!'

Charlie cringed. Why couldn't her mother be clean, pristine and cool like Mrs Williams?

'I love your mum,' Polly whispered. 'She's so real.'

What Polly saw in her mother that she herself didn't see was a question that Charlie would have to ask her later. Maybe everyone thought their own mum was embarrassing.

'*Right!*' Caroline Bass clapped her hands together. 'Who's for orange squash with loads of ice, and a slice of green pea cake? It's a new recipe. I thought it would be nice and summery.'

'I'll certainly have a glass of something cold, but I think I'll pass on the cake.' Mrs Williams smiled. 'I don't want to ruin the memory of the beetroot and apple rock cakes you brought round last week. We so love your experimental cooking.'

Polly and Charlie tried to stifle their giggles and sneaked out of the room, leaving their mothers to discuss alternative recipes and therapeutic exercise.

'Do you want to come out and see Noddy?' asked Charlie.

'Oh, yes please,' said Polly. 'I've been so looking forward to being near horses again. Dad won't let me in his racing yard in case I get kicked and Munchkin is on permanent loan to my cousin.' She lowered her eyes to avoid Charlie's gaze. Charlie shook her head in disappointment. She wished there was something she could do to help.

'You've got a real knack with horses and I think sometimes they know that they have to be gentle with you. Remember how Noddy stopped snorting when he came towards you at Ascot? How he suddenly calmed down and didn't pull backwards when you held his lead rein?'

Polly sighed. 'My parents think that was just a fluke. Mum said she nearly had a heart attack when everyone else had run out of the way and I was standing there on my own. She thinks I couldn't move fast enough, but to be honest, I would have stood still even before the accident. It's the most sensible thing to do.'

Charlie knew her friend was right, but it still took an incredible amount of courage and calmness of mind to stay still when a panicked horse was charging around.

'He's so different now,' Charlie said as they made their way towards the field, with Boris the Border terrier trotting along behind them. 'He's really settled down and it's as if the racing part of his mind has just switched off.'

The girls approached the paddock fence and Charlie called out to Noddy and Percy who were at the far end of the field in the shade. Percy whinnied at Charlie, hoping for food, and starting ambling down the hill towards the barn. Noddy followed the pony faithfully. Charlie watched them carefully as they walked towards the fence, checking they were both sound.

'Look – Noddy's got fatter and he's so laid-back.' She grinned at Polly. 'I think he's enjoying the lazy lifestyle!'

Noble Warrior walked straight up to Polly and

stuck his head over the fence so that she could stroke him.

She leaned over and brushed his nose. 'Oh, it feels so lovely!' She kissed the velvety curve of Noddy's cheek and inhaled. 'I'd forgotten how wonderful they smell and how soft their skin is.'

Noble Warrior was a thoroughbred. His skin was more delicate and his hair finer than his tubby, furry friend Percy's. Percy, who never missed an opportunity to eat, poked his head through the gap

in the fence and frisked the pockets of Charlie's shorts in the hope of a treat.

'You're in luck, greedy one.' She laughed and pulled out two carrots. She handed one to Polly to give to Noble Warrior, and before she could even stretch out to offer the other one to Percy, he had snatched it from her.

'Some things never change!' said Polly with a grin.

Charlie took the opportunity to apply more sunscreen to Percy's pink-skinned nose, while Polly looked more closely at Noble Warrior.

'If I'm being honest, I think he needs a bit of conditioning.' Polly pointed her crutch at his tummy as she leaned on the fence. 'I don't mean to be rude, but that's quite a belly he's got there!'

It was true. A casual passer-by might have thought Noddy was a mare in foal rather than a Derby winner enjoying his retirement.

'Maybe we should start exercising him?' Charlie suggested. 'What do you think?'

Polly stroked Noddy's head again. 'I think you'd

like that, wouldn't you, fella? It's no fun doing nothing at all. We all need a bit of a challenge in our lives, something to aim at, something to work for. It'll make you stronger, inside and out.'

Charlie was pleased to see her friend happy. She knew how frustrated Polly had been by the numerous trips to hospital and the endless cycle of preparing for and recovering from an operation.

'I don't think I could bear to live a life without horses,' Polly sighed. 'I wish my parents knew how miserable it makes me to have to stay away from them.'

Noddy sniffed Polly's hair and nudged her gently with his nose.

'I think they're trying to keep you safe,' Charlie replied. She saw tears spring up in Polly's eyes. Polly buried her face in Noddy's neck to hide them.

'I don't know what to do,' Polly said, her voice muffled. 'It's like living in a prison with one or other of my parents always lurking, scared that I might trip or catch myself on a door, rushing towards me to hold my arm, or moving things out of my way. They won't even let me get a *kitten* because they're terrified it will scratch me or make me fall over!'

Charlie felt a flush of anger on Polly's behalf. 'I could kill them!' she spat.

Polly looked surprised. 'I think that's a bit extreme. They annoy me, but I don't want to kill them.' She paused. 'I'd be pretty sad without any parents.'

'No!' Charlie exclaimed. 'Not your *parents*. The *kidnappers*. The men who are doing time in jail right now. They completely changed your life and Noddy's and now you're both in limbo, not knowing what to do with yourselves.'

Noble Warrior jerked his head up at Charlie's raised voice. The sharp movement knocked Polly off balance and she wobbled, trying to use her left leg to keep herself upright. It collapsed beneath her.

'Ow!' Her face twisted in agony as she hit the ground.

Charlie rushed to her side and slid her arm

underneath her friend's shoulders to help her sit up.

'Are you OK? I'm so sorry.'

Polly gritted her teeth. Her eyes scrunched up in concentration, and after a few heavy breaths, her lips started to move, but no sound came out.

'*Noddy, you naughty boy!*' Charlie turned to her ex-racehorse to admonish him. 'You can't behave like that.'

'Eight, nine, *ten*.' Polly exhaled loudly.

'What?' Charlie asked.

'It's what I do when it really hurts. It comes in waves and I know it will pass so I count to ten and sometimes back down again until it feels better.'

Noble Warrior whickered gently. He hung his head over the fence, his ears flicking backwards and forwards and his eyes focused on Polly.

'Don't be cross with him.' Polly started to sit up slowly. 'He didn't do it on purpose. Just look at him – he's genuinely sorry!'

Percy, meanwhile, didn't glance their way. He

was too busy, his head stretching under the bottom rail of the fence, trying desperately to reach a few blades of grass that hadn't been burnt brown by the sun.

Polly laughed weakly. 'Percy would probably knock me over and trample me for a lump of sugar! But I don't think Noddy meant to do it.'

Noddy stretched out his neck and sniffed at Polly.

'It's OK, fella. I'll live.' Polly leaned on Charlie for support and stiffly clambered to her feet. Charlie put the crutch in her hand and offered her arm for support on the other side.

Polly waved it away.

'I'm fine,' she said sharply. 'It happens all the time.'

She hobbled towards Noddy and reached out her right arm to stroke his nose. 'I know it was an accident. You didn't mean to hurt me. I'm just not as stable as I used to be, that's the problem. We've both been a bit scrambled, but hey, we'll learn to get on with it, won't we?'

She scratched Noddy behind the ears and he lowered his head appreciatively.

Polly turned to look defiantly at Charlie. 'Don't tell Mum.'

Chapter 2

'There's an email from Joe!' Larry ran across the farmyard towards them waving his iPad, one of the many gadgets he had bought with his share of Noble Warrior's Derby prize money.

Joe had joined their family as a farmhand, but his riding skill and his rapport with Noble Warrior had earned him the right to apply for a jockey's licence and ride him in the Derby. His horsemanship had caught the eye of Europe's leading trainer, Seamus

O'Reilly, who had offered him his dream job in Ireland.

'What does he say?' asked Polly eagerly. Charlie grinned at her friend's pink cheeks. Polly had always had a soft spot for Joe.

'Come over here and I'll tell you.'

Larry plonked himself down cross-legged on the grass under the broad branches of the copper beech tree that gave shelter and shade on both sides of the fence. Noble Warrior and Percy followed on their side while Larry leaned against the tree trunk for support and rested his iPad on his knees. Charlie moved a tree stump that her father had shaped into a stool so that Polly could sit comfortably. With Charlie's help, she lowered herself gingerly on to the stump. Charlie could feel her wince, but Polly shook her head to warn her not to say anything.

'I'll read it to you,' Larry said self-importantly. Boris lay beside him with his hind legs stretched out flat behind him like a spatchcock chicken.

'*Hi, team,*' Larry read. '*I miss you all very much, but things are going great here. Mr O'Reilly lets me ride all of the good horses in their work, so twice a week is like a race day as I switch from one horse to the other –'*

'Sounds intense,' said Charlie.

Larry raised his hand in mock outrage. 'If you're going to interrupt, I won't bother.'

Charlie and Polly looked at each other and giggled.

'Can I continue?' Larry asked.

'Go ahead, sire,' Charlie replied.

'*Little Lion Man, who you'll remember from Derby Day, has blossomed into a really nice four-year-old. I'm hoping I might be allowed to ride him in the Irish Champion Stakes, which is a huge race over here.*

'*What's happening your end? I hope the cows are doing OK. Give Taylor Swift a head-rub from me and say hello to the pigs. I hope the chickens are surviving their dance lessons.*'

Larry slammed the iPad on his knees.

'Surviving?' he said. 'I think you'll find, Joe Butler, that the chickens like their dancing very much and lay considerably more eggs after a

21

samba class than they ever did before.'

'Get back to the email, Anton du Peck,' Charlie laughed.

Larry puffed out his cheeks and carried on reading.

'*Love to Boris and to all of you, but especially to Noddy and Percy. I hope you're all having fun in the sun. I'll try to come and see you when I'm over for one of the big meetings.*'

'Oh, I hope so,' Polly whispered.

'That's about it. There's a nice photo of him riding out at Seamus O'Reilly's – look at all those white rails and those beautifully mown gallops. It's just like being at a racecourse. That must have cost some serious dosh!'

He handed the iPad to Charlie so that she and Polly could see. Charlie slid her finger up the page.

'Oh, look!' she said. 'There's a PS.'

'What does it say?' asked Larry and Polly together.

Charlie paused, unsure whether to read it out loud.

'Go on!' Polly urged her.

'It says, *PS Have you got Polly and Noddy together yet? They'd make a great team. I think they'd look after each other.*'

Polly blushed bright red and stared at her shoes.

Larry scrunched up his face. 'Eh? What's he on about?'

'Oh, nothing,' Charlie said quickly. 'He said something similar in the paddock at Ascot. Joe thinks they've got a special bond.'

'We haven't,' Polly said quickly. 'I was just lucky.'

She looked across at Noble Warrior munching contentedly in the field.

'I don't think Joe realizes . . .' Polly said quietly. 'That neither of us are quite up to it.'

Polly bowed her head.

'Yet,' Charlie whispered.

'Right, girls. Gotta go!' Larry jumped up, grabbing his iPad from his little sister. 'People to see, things to do, chickens to train.'

He did a pirouette and kicked his heels as he headed off for the chicken shed.

Noble Warrior and Percy had drifted away up to

the top of the field, towards the woods. There was a path leading down to the river and, although the level had dropped, there was still enough cool fresh water to drink and bathe their legs.

'If they're going into the shade, I guess we'd better do the same,' Charlie said. Polly winced as she stood up from her tree-stump stool. 'Do you need some painkillers?' Charlie asked.

'No,' Polly replied through gritted teeth. 'It's really nothing. I'm used to it.'

They wandered back to the farmhouse to find that Mrs Williams had finally been persuaded by Mrs Bass to leave her daughter in their hands. The list of which pills she had to take and exercises she had to do was stuck to the fridge door with a magnet.

Charlie was taking a look at it when Harry came flying into the room. He was wearing the latest Southampton home kit and matching shorts. He slid across the stone floor in his socks, waving a piece of paper at them.

'It's worked!' he shouted. 'We've got a booking!'

24

He came to a standstill by the kitchen sink where he held the piece of paper aloft with both hands.

'What are you on about?' Charlie feared this was another of her brothers' wild money-making schemes.

'Noddy has been asked to open a new supermarket in Andover. Isn't that great? The local paper will be there and I bet we can get the *Racing Post* to send a photographer – and then who knows where it will lead?' Harry looked at the piece of paper again and flicked it with his finger. 'I knew people would read that blog. I *knew* it!'

'What blog?' Charlie asked, frowning. 'What have you been up to?'

'I know about the blog,' Polly interjected excitedly. 'My dad told me about it! *The Diary of an Ex-Racehorse.*'

'Yeah,' Harry said proudly. 'I tugged at the

heartstrings a bit, made out Noddy was like an actor who couldn't get a job.' He shook the piece of paper. 'And here we have it – a new stage and a new audience and five hundred pounds guaranteed as an appearance fee! I've printed off the booking and I might get it framed. This is the start of a whole new life for . . .' He paused and held his arms wide. 'Noble Warrior – the racehorse who opens supermarkets!'

'No,' Charlie said flatly.

Harry stared at her. 'Whaddya mean "no"? *LARRY!*' He shouted through the door. 'Larry, get in here and back me up.'

'I think it's demeaning,' Charlie explained. 'I don't want him being poked and prodded and having to walk down the pasta aisle for a photo shoot. It's not what he should be doing.'

'Well, you can get all high and mighty if you like,' Larry said as he walked into the kitchen with a file in his hand. 'But I've got the figures here and it still costs money to feed Noddy and Percy, plus we've got the vet's bills and the farrier. *And* the insurance premiums have rocketed after the kidnap.'

He put the file on the table and turned the pages so Charlie could see the costs laid out in black and white.

'Now all he's going to do is soak up what's left of his Derby winnings.'

Larry paused as he showed her the predicted figures in the years to come and the large red minus sign in front of them. He took a big breath that filled the kitchen as he sighed it out.

'Look, Charlie, we've got to be realistic about this. I heard Mum and Dad discussing options the other night and I've gotta tell you, it's not good.'

'What do you mean?' Charlie's heart jumped into her throat.

'I *mean* that they can't afford it. His racing days are behind him so there's no prize money. The only way he could sing for his supper is to go off to stud and be a stallion, but you don't want him to leave. Now you're saying he can't go out in public, so here's the big question – how *do* you think he should earn his keep?'

Charlie shrugged her shoulders. 'I don't know. But there's got to be a better way than opening supermarkets.'

'There is!' exclaimed Harry. 'He can go to weddings, do school appearances, turn on the Christmas lights, even do a fashion shoot if we get the right sort of publicity. There is literally no limit.'

'Literally?' said Charlie. 'I think you'll find there *literally* is a limit and that limit would be me.'

'I don't understand why you've got so snobbish about it all, Charlie Bass,' said Larry, snapping the folder shut. 'Red Rum did all this stuff and earned money for years after he won the Grand National. He even turned on the lights at Blackpool Tower.'

'And that was back when Blackpool was buzzing all year round, not just when *Strictly* comes to town!' added Harry.

'If you mention *Strictly* one more time, I'll make you . . .' Charlie hesitated. She knew she couldn't threaten her brothers with violence because they were bigger than her and anyway, she didn't believe in it. 'I'll make you . . . eat the rest of Mum's rock cakes.'

As threats went, it wasn't exactly a spine-chiller. Harry and Larry started laughing. Even Polly joined in and Charlie was forced to allow herself a smile.

'Seriously, though, I don't want Noddy going off to open supermarkets. It's not what he won the Derby for.'

'I know that.' Harry walked towards her and put an arm round her shoulder. He had shot up in height in the last year and towered over his sister. 'I just don't think he should sit out in a field doing nothing.' He spoke gently. 'He has fans and they want to see him. And he's an athlete! He should look like one.'

'It's a weird thing,' said Larry. 'We started the blog and put up photos of Noddy in the field, but after a while it was same old, same old. Suddenly it was like I was in his head and it just felt a bit . . . sad.'

Polly looked thoughtful. 'My dad read one of the blog posts to me and it made me cry. It was like a heart-breaking monologue from a faded star. Just last summer he achieved the impossible and now he's a hermit.'

'Well, if you put it like that,' Charlie said. 'I guess it is a bit tragic.' She sat down at the kitchen table and ushered the others to join her. 'OK,' she said. 'I take your point. We all know he can't stay in the field with Percy forever. So what are the options?'

'Can't you at least *consider* the supermarket?' Harry said.

'They know Percy will have to come too,' Larry added. 'We explained that they come together as a Buy-One-Get-One-Free deal and they said that was what they were all about. They say BOGOF is their most popular offer.'

Polly was listening carefully. 'It *would* give us a reason to get him fit again,' she said. 'He can't turn up for a photo shoot unless he's looking his best – and it will be good for him to have something to concentrate on again. We could start lunging him this evening when it's a bit cooler. I can help if you like?'

Charlie looked at Polly. If it made her friend want to get involved, then it couldn't be the worst idea. 'Absolutely,' she said, her voice more decisive than she felt.

'Hey, kids, everything OK?' Mrs Bass pulled bits of straw from her hair as she walked into the kitchen. 'Any of you fancy a rock cake?'

'*No!*' they all said at once.

As the sun started to dip in the sky and the trees cast long, cool shadows, Polly helped Charlie plait together reams of baler twine to make one strong length of rope. The two friends sat next to each other on a bale of hay and let their hands work as they talked through their plans.

'I think the trick is to get him supple, build up his muscles so that he looks the part,' Charlie said, folding one piece of orange string over the other. 'He needs to develop strength in his neck and hold his head so he looks pretty, like that poster I've got of Charlotte Dujardin on Valegro.'

'We'll have to groom him every day,' Polly

pointed out. 'His coat will only get its shine back if we work at it. That way his neck and his quarters will really glimmer in the photos.'

They combined one length of plaited string with another.

'Where did the boys go?' Polly asked.

'Oh, I don't know. They've been busy putting up new security cameras. After the kidnap we all got a bit jittery. About *everything* that we value.' Charlie ran her hand through her short hair. 'I mean, I don't think anyone would steal the pigs or the chickens, and the cows would kick them to death if they tried to separate them! But I think Mum was worried that the new farm machinery might be a target, so she got the boys to put up a few more cameras. Mind you, I saw them with a pot of white paint about an hour ago and I have no idea how that's connected.' She stood up. 'There. You hold that end and I'll see how much we've got.'

She walked ten paces away and found that there was enough string to stretch, with a bit left over –

'Just under ten metres,' she announced.

'A diameter of twenty metres, then,' said Polly.

'Yep,' said Charlie. 'A twenty-metre circle is perfect to lunge him. We can keep him tight until he gets the hang of it and then let him go bigger if we can get him into a nice steady canter.'

'Looks good to me!' Polly pushed herself up on her crutch. 'I remember Joe telling me he'd tried to get Noddy to do some dressage as a way of making him better balanced. He said he was a natural.'

'Speaking of balance,' Charlie said, 'haven't you got to do some exercises? Your mum won't let you come again unless we follow her rules!'

'It's usually Pilates,' Polly explained. 'I've got to work on my core strength so that my body can manage the lack of movement in my left side. The doctors say that if I can work on my core, the left leg won't be such a drag and my right side won't hurt so much from taking all the pressure.' She sighed. 'I guess it makes sense, but I can't tell you how boring it is!'

Charlie caught her eye and they laughed together.

'Still,' Polly continued, 'I'm in a much better place than I was after the accident and that's how they've told me to think about it. The accident itself was day zero and every day after that can only be compared to day zero. It's no use thinking about how I was *before*.'

'Exactly,' Charlie said.

As the girls strolled out towards the field, they spotted Charlie's brothers walking with long strides in the bottom-right corner. Harry had a new streak of white across the front of his Southampton football shirt and Larry had specks of white dotted all over the grey T-shirt he'd been wearing throughout the summer. They were holding wooden markers with letters on them.

'Forty paces down the long side and twenty on the short side,' Harry shouted, clearly in charge. 'Try to keep straight, Larry! It's important.'

They placed white boards at each corner of a slightly wonky rectangle on the grass.

'That's where *F* goes!' Harry shouted at his

younger brother. 'No, not *M*. *F* comes before *A* on the right-hand corner.'

'Who made up this daft letter system?' Larry shouted back. 'It doesn't make any sense!'

'*A King Eats His Cold Meat Before Fast*.' The girls were close enough now to hear Harry talking to himself as he checked the letters round the edge of the large rectangle. 'It doesn't rhyme and why would the king be fasting anyway? It's a stupid way of remembering something that someone clearly made up when they were drunk.'

Charlie immediately recognized the rectangle and its random lettering. She and Polly looked at each other and said together, in surprise, 'It's a dressage arena!'

Harry placed the letter H in the top left corner, after E and before C.

'*M* should go opposite – in the other corner. I think that's right.' Harry took twenty paces from C towards A, more or less in a straight line. '*X* is here in the middle so I'll just paint it on the grass.'

The two brothers met in the centre of their

makeshift arena to survey their work. They nodded in satisfaction and high fived each other.

'Hey, Charlie, Polly, come and have a look!' Harry yelled, beckoning with his arm. 'We've made you a present!'

Polly and Charlie rushed over as quickly as they could.

'How on earth –?'

'I looked it up on the internet,' Harry interrupted Charlie excitedly. 'I wanted to find the best way to get a horse ready for a photo shoot and this is what came up. Dressage!'

'Wow!' Polly said. 'I'm impressed. You look like you've got the measurements right and all the letters in the correct order. Apart from the paint on your shirt, you've done a pretty tidy job.'

'What paint?' Harry looked down and howled. *'Not on my new shirt!'*

'Don't worry,' sniggered Larry. 'They'll probably bring out a new shirt next season with a white stripe across the middle and you'll be well ahead of the game.'

'I wouldn't expect any sympathy from you.' Harry pushed his brother away. 'Just because I don't wear exactly the same shirt every single day of the week, every week of the summer!'

Larry pushed him back and soon they were throwing each other to the ground.

'Guys!' Charlie didn't want a full-scale fight. There was too much work to do. 'Don't start all that again. You've done a fantastic job here and I'm really grateful.'

Larry rose to his feet and brushed off the dust. Harry looked a little sheepish.

''S nothing much,' he mumbled. 'Just, you know, trying to help.'

'Well, it's perfect,' Charlie said. 'Polly and I were just talking about getting Noble Warrior fit again. We were thinking of a kind of mind-and-body fitness programme.'

''Zackly,' said Larry. 'We could write about it for the blog!'

'That's a good idea,' Harry agreed. 'I can do little videos of Noddy learning to do that fancy dressage stuff when they lift their feet up and it's like they're . . .'

He paused and looked at his brother. They came to the same conclusion at the same time.

'*Dancing!*' they shouted together.

They grabbed each other's hands and started jumping up and down on the spot. Then Harry ran towards his sister and spun her round, flinging her across his arm so that she bent backwards. Larry jumped towards Polly, who threw her crutch down as he lifted her feet off the ground and spun her round him.

'*Careful!*' Harry shouted.

Polly was laughing as Larry gently put her feet back on the ground.

'Don't worry. It didn't hurt at all!' she said delightedly.

'This is the chance we've been waiting for!' Larry explained as he handed Polly back her crutch. 'We can work on the music and choreograph the routines and you two can do the horsey bit. This is *classic* material for the blog and I think it will open up a whole new raft of opportunities for Noddy.'

Charlie was still smiling as she said, 'Let's not tango before we can trot in a circle, OK? We're doing this for Noddy, remember, not for us. It's not about making money – so don't you even start on that.'

The boys looked at each other and winked.

'I think it's important we give him a challenge that will stretch him,' Polly added. 'Make him feel he's trying to achieve something others thought he couldn't do, give him a sense of purpose. That's how he'll feel like a champion again.'

As if he had heard them talking about him, Noddy appeared behind Polly and put his head over her shoulder, allowing her to lean back into his chest. She put her hand up and stroked the length of his nose.

'Shall we give it a go?' Charlie held up the headcollar and home-made lunge rope.

'No time like the present,' Polly said, still running

her hand down Noddy's long nose. 'This will be the making of you,' she whispered in his ear. 'This is the start – day one of a whole new life.'

Chapter 3

Charlie held up the headcollar and Noddy bowed his head to accept it. She tied the plaited rope to the loop below his chin and led him into the middle of the arena. Percy was following a little way behind, nibbling at the few patches of grass that weren't brown. He looked up every so often to check what his friend was up to.

'It's OK, Perce, I won't make you do it!' Charlie called out to him. 'I know it's not your thing.'

She showed Noble Warrior the shape of the circle she wanted him to make, leading him round with a short rein. Then she positioned herself in the centre of the arena, her feet on the painted X. She loosened the rope and clicked her teeth. Noddy began to walk in a circle wider and wider round her.

'Good boy, that's the way. Now *trot on*!' Charlie was strong and confident in her command and clicked her tongue on the roof of her mouth as she said it.

Noble Warrior moved forward into trot, keeping his head low and his stride level. Boris barked encouragement from the sidelines and Noble Warrior gave a little squeal of excitement and raised his back legs in a buck.

'He's full of beans!' called Polly. 'I think he's enjoying it.'

Charlie worked him for ten minutes going left-handed before letting him walk and changing the rein. Then she worked him for ten minutes going right-handed, watching his shoulders and neck become more flexible as he got used to the idea of going in a circle in a steady trot that forced him to use the power in his hindquarters.

'He's spent his life galloping in a straight line and then learning to come round Tattenham Corner at full speed. This is using his muscles in a very different way,' Charlie said as she urged him forward.

Noble Warrior responded willingly. His hooves snapped up with every stride and his hind legs thrust underneath him, making him look as if he was on springs.

'I think he could do with some music,' Harry murmured to his younger brother. 'I can just see those hooves drumming to the beat and I think it would help his rhythm.'

'We've got those Bluetooth speakers we bought for the chickens. They would do the trick,' Larry said in a stage whisper.

Polly was leaning on the fence just behind them. She poked her crutch at Larry. 'I can hear you.'

'Don't you think it needs a bit of pizzazz?' said

Harry. 'Otherwise it's just trotting round in circles and, to be totally honest, that ain't gonna keep any of us on the edge of our seats.'

'Funnily enough,' said Polly, 'you're not being completely stupid.'

Harry raised his eyebrows in mock outrage.

'Freestyle dressage is all about the music,' Polly said. 'I remember when Charlotte Dujardin won her gold medal at the London Olympics, the music was all this patriotic stuff like "Land of Hope and Glory" and it made all the difference. The crowd loved it and the judges gave her top marks.'

'Do you think horses can hear a tune?' asked Larry.

'Absolutely. They definitely move in time with the music and there are some horses who prefer a certain type of music.'

'You're joking,' said Harry.

'Honestly!' Polly looked back towards Noble Warrior and Charlie still working hard in the arena. His hooves were creating a track in a circle round her.

'Some won't do much for classical music, but will really turn on the style for a pop song. I've read about it and seen it on YouTube. I'll show you.'

Larry shook his head in disbelief. 'Who knew? We've been slogging away with those darned chickens and all along the dancing shoes were waiting for this fella!'

'Whoa, lad, that'll do.' In the arena, Charlie slowed Noble Warrior right down and let him walk towards her. His body was glistening with sweat. She patted him on the neck.

'That's enough for this evening. We don't want to put you off by overdoing it.'

Charlie was amazed that such a slow and short training session could make him sweat so much. He wasn't puffing like he did when he finished a gallop in his racing days, but he had clearly been working hard.

'I think he enjoyed that,' she said to Polly and her brothers as she led Noddy towards the barn. 'I think he quite likes the attention as well as the exercise. I'll just put a hose on him before he goes back out in the field.'

Harry and Larry turned to head back to the farmhouse.

'Hey, thanks for the arena!' Charlie shouted after them.

'*Teamwork makes the Dream Work!*' they shouted back in unison.

Polly smiled at Charlie. 'I don't know where they get their slogans, but hey, they aren't all bad,' she said.

'I know. They're idiot brothers, but at least they're *my* idiot brothers.'

Charlie walked Noble Warrior back towards the barn. The sun-baked ground was rough and uneven. As they passed the straw bales that Harry had built to make practice starting stalls before the Derby, Charlie looked over her shoulder and saw Polly stumble.

'Don't wait, I'll be fine.' Polly banged her crutch on the ground. 'It's just this stupid leg doesn't want to pick itself up.' Her face was flushed and her teeth gritted.

Charlie hesitated, unsure whether to carry on and not make a fuss or wait for her friend. She circled back and let Noddy sniff the ground. He started pawing with his hooves at the dust and a cloud of brown lifted off like smoke.

'I think he wants to roll,' Charlie said to Polly, who hobbled closer and leaned against the straw bales for support.

Noble Warrior had dug a small trench in the ground and now he was kneeling down into it, lowering his front end first and then his bottom. Charlie held on to the rope, keeping it well out of the way of his flailing hooves as he rolled on to his back and flung his body one way and then the other.

'My dad always says it's lucky if they flip themselves right over,' Polly said. 'He reckons it means it's a horse who will win a race. I don't know why, as you wouldn't have thought the ability to roll would have any bearing on your speed! But Dad also salutes magpies and thinks going under a railway bridge while a train is passing above means

he'll train a winner, so it's all relative.'

Noddy stretched his neck out in the dirt and moved it from side to side, scratching it on the ground. Percy trotted over to see what was going on, hoping there might be food involved.

'He's just having a post-workout massage,' Charlie explained to Percy. 'If you did any work, you could have one too.'

Noble Warrior turned himself right over on to his other side and then let out a big breath of air before sitting up like a dog. He looked pleased with himself. Charlie held the rope loosely and gave him time to raise himself back up to his full height. He shook his head, his neck and then his whole body as bits of dust flew into the air.

'I wish I could do that,' Polly murmured. 'It looks more fun than Pilates.'

Charlie patted his neck and smiled. Noble Warrior whinnied softly at Percy, who walked over to be next to him.

'He's definitely finding his confidence again after the kidnap,' Charlie said. It was nearly a year ago now, but she could still remember how he used to jump at any loud noise, even months after the event.

'I'll never forget the sound he made when they came speeding past me on the road.' Polly shuddered as she recalled the seconds before Munchkin reared and sent her crashing into the tarmac. 'Noddy was thrashing and kicking in the back and his whinny sounded like a scream. He was terrified.'

Noble Warrior moved closer to Polly as she

spoke, as if drawn in by her voice. He reached out his nose to her and she stroked him. He lowered his head and nudged her, willing her to move herself higher on the straw bales. They were arranged in steps so that it wasn't difficult for her to climb on to the first one. Noble Warrior nudged her again.

'I think he wants you to go higher,' Charlie said.

'Maybe he's got some dust on his back that I can brush off for him,' Polly suggested as she dropped her crutch to the floor and carefully moved on to the second bale. She was level with his back and ran her hand along it from the withers to the top of his tail.

'That should do it,' she said.

Noble Warrior turned his head and looked at her before moving himself slightly so that he was parallel to the straw bales.

'I think he wants you to get on him,' Charlie whispered, holding his rope a little more tightly.

Polly shook her head. 'I can't. What if I fell off? Mum would kill me.' Noble Warrior looked round at her again and pushed himself closer to the bales. 'He's got no saddle on. I'll never be able to hold myself in position.' She took a deep breath. *'I'm scared*. There! I said it. Mum and Dad are right – I've lost my bottle. I wouldn't be able to ride again, even if they let me.'

Noble Warrior stayed stock-still in front of the straw bales where Polly was standing. She sighed loudly and he looked round at her once more.

'It's OK,' Charlie said softly. 'No one's going to make you do anything you don't want to. I reckon *Noddy* thinks it would be easier to ride back to the stables than to walk.' Charlie knew that all Polly had to do was lift her right leg over his back and she'd be sitting on top of him. 'Your mum isn't here. She'll never know. Take my riding hat.' She unbuckled it and passed it over.

'But how will I balance?' Polly's voice trembled.

Charlie positioned herself on the other side of Noble Warrior's shoulder, ready to keep her friend steady and hold on to the leading rein. 'I guess that's down to your core strength.' She smiled encouragingly. 'Think of it as an alternative therapy. Like Pilates – but more fun!'

Polly started to count to ten and when she got to nine she put her left hand on to Noble Warrior's mane. She faced away from his head and lifted her right leg. Her left leg wobbled and almost buckled. She fell backwards against the top straw bale.

'I can't do it!'

Charlie dropped the lead rein to the floor and stood in front of Noble Warrior. She spoke to him earnestly and firmly. 'Right, Noddy, this seems to be your idea so you'd better help make it work. Don't move an inch, OK? Not one inch while I help Polly get on.'

Noble Warrior bowed his head as if he understood and didn't move a muscle. Charlie scrambled up the two bales to be on the same level as Polly. She offered herself as support, helping her friend keep her balance as she tried to swing her right leg over again.

'One, two, *three*!' Charlie said as they worked together. One final shove on Polly's bottom and she was up. It was probably stupid, but it made them both laugh out loud.

'I've always wanted to ride a Derby winner!' grinned Polly. 'I guess that dream has come true.'

'Hold tight to his mane and try to sit up tall,' Charlie urged as she scrambled down from the makeshift mounting block to take the lead rein.

'Good boy, Noddy. You kept your word. Now let's walk as steadily as you can.'

Charlie looked up at Polly, who was smiling and looking around. Her back and hips moved in rhythm with Noble Warrior's stride.

'How does it feel?' Charlie asked.

'*Magical*. It feels amazing to move without having to worry about whether I'll trip or stumble.'

Polly looked from side to side, taking in the view, and she glanced down at Charlie.

'I feel free,' she said.

Those three words meant the world to Charlie. She wanted to bottle this moment and take it out whenever things got tough at school.

It was only a short walk and they didn't go very fast, but it was enough.

When they got to the barn, Charlie helped Polly slide gently to the floor and ran back to get her crutch. As she ran, she thought about all the things *she* could do without fear or worry. She could run, she could walk, she could jump on Percy from the ground and she didn't have to hesitate or work out the risks. She could just do it. She had taken all that for granted.

When she returned, she found Polly with her arms round Noble Warrior, her face buried in his neck. Charlie couldn't hear what she was saying, but when Polly drew her head back, Charlie could see her friend was crying.

Charlie's heart jumped into her throat. 'Are you upset? I'm so sorry, we shouldn't have done that. I didn't mean to make you cry.'

'Don't say that,' Polly replied, sniffing. 'These are happy tears. You and Noddy have just given me the best day since day zero. Maybe even the best day ever.'

Charlie smiled with relief as she handed Polly her crutch. She turned on the tap, sending water pumping through the hose, which made Noble Warrior spook.

'He thinks it's a giant snake! And you know what it's like with thoroughbreds – they can be perfect gents one minute and perfect fools the next.'

She aimed the water at his back and sprayed off all the dust, as well as the clear outline that Polly's legs had left behind.

'Girls! Are you coming inside?' Charlie's mother was calling from the farmyard. 'Polly's due to take her pills at seven and it's quarter past already. Supper's on the table.'

'Coming, Mum!' Charlie shouted back.

They finished hosing off Noble Warrior, ran a scraper over his body to take off the excess water and took him back to the field. Charlie slipped off the headcollar and they watched him trot over to Percy, lowering his head between his knees as he went.

'I think he's got the dressage bug,' Polly laughed.

'He's even practising in his own time.'

'We can give it another go tomorrow, if you like?'

Polly put her head on one side and widened her eyes, but she didn't answer. Charlie left the idea hanging in the air. They could sleep on it.

'Have you done your exercises, Polly?' Charlie's mother asked as they walked into the kitchen.

'Yes, Mrs Bass. We found a new exercise that works really well.' Polly winked at Charlie as she spoke. 'I can feel my core muscles getting stronger already!'

Chapter 4

The Bass family's old brick farmhouse with stone floors certainly had its benefits. It may have been chilly in the winter, but in this, the hottest of summers, it was staying nice and cool. The next morning, Charlie, Polly and the boys sat round the big old wooden table in the kitchen. They were watching Charlotte Dujardin's freestyle dressage routine from London 2012.

'See there, when he looks as if he's prancing?'

Charlie pointed to the screen. 'That's called passage.' She pronounced the word as if it was in French – *pas-arge*. 'It's an elevated trot so the knees have to come right up. It's all about showing power. You see how the legs seem to hang in the air before they come down again? It's brilliant. And then here –' she pressed Pause on the screen, pointed, and then let it play on – 'you see she's keeping him on the one spot as he trots. That's called a piaffe.'

'Gosh, it really is like dancing,' said Harry.

'And when you hear it with the music –' Larry turned up the volume – 'you can tell how good it is. Valegro is trotting in time with the beat. Now, that's clever! And there, where he goes into extended trot for the James Bond music – it's brilliant.'

Charlie never imagined she could sit and discuss dressage with her brothers. They had always teased her about her fascination with equestrian sport and mocked her for wanting to watch Olympia at Christmas time or the Grand Prix at the World Equestrian Games. Now they were engrossed.

'This would be so cool for the blog,' Larry said under his breath to Harry.

'Get outta my head!' his older brother replied. 'I was already planning this wicked film sequence where you only see his feet or his neck or his ears and then, like, a week later, we reveal that it's actually Noble Warrior doing dressage.'

'Do you reckon the aisles of the supermarket are wide enough for him to do a piaffe?'

'Look at this bit. He's skipping!' Harry said hastily, spotting Charlie's expression.

Larry rewound the film so he could watch the flying changes again. Every other stride, Valegro changed his lead leg from left to right to left to right again. Charlotte Dujardin barely moved at all apart from a tiny adjustment with her leg that shifted her hips from one side to the other. Her hands stayed level and her upper body rock solid.

'Now *that* is core strength.' Polly was impressed.

Charlotte Dujardin came to the end of her routine, bowed her head to the judges and smiled. The crowd started cheering and the commentator sounded as if he was in tears, his voice cracked with emotion. Charlotte dropped the reins and patted Valegro on both sides of his neck. He transformed instantly from a high-class performer, ready and alert for the next move, to being an old dobbin coming home from a hack.

Larry sniffed and wiped away a tear. 'It's beautiful.' Charlie wasn't sure whether he was mocking her.

Harry dug him in the ribs. 'Don't be so soft,' he scoffed. 'You knew she won the gold medal before we even started watching. We couldn't have missed it if we tried, what with Charlie banging on and on about it. It was all she would talk about when she was six.'

Larry sniffed again. 'I was *not* crying,' he protested. 'I'm getting a cold.'

Charlie took the laptop and tapped away on the screen. 'There's something else I want to show you,' she said. She pressed Play on the video. Polly leaned in.

On the screen was another dressage test. The

arena in Greenwich looked the same and the purple banners said 'London 2012'. The rider raised an arm to signal for the music to start.

'Wow, what a beautiful horse,' Polly said as they watched the woman and her horse enter the arena. Then she noticed something.

'She hasn't got any stirrups,' she said, pointing to the screen. 'Why would you make it even harder for yourself like that?'

They watched the rider ask her horse to move forward into canter. The stunning jet-black animal kept his neck arched and smoothly changed his stride into an even, rhythmic canter. His tail flowed out behind him as the rider sat tall and proud. Polly was mesmerized.

After a minute, Charlie spoke. 'She can't walk.'

'Don't be ridiculous,' Polly retorted. 'You can't ride like that if you can't use your legs.'

'Look carefully – she's talking to her horse. She uses verbal commands and if you look at her bottom, that's where all the strength is coming from.'

Polly shook her head in disbelief.

'I looked it up,' Charlie continued. 'She's called Natasha Baker and the horse is Cabral. When she was only fourteen months old she got a virus called transverse my-ah . . .' She paused and looked at something she had written in her notebook. 'Mya-lye-tiss, that's it. Transverse myelitis. It's known as TM. It's a neurological condition so it comes from the brain, but it affects the spinal cord and makes it swell up.'

Polly couldn't take her eyes off the screen as she watched Natasha and Cabral do the most extravagant extended trot diagonally across the arena.

'She had permanent nerve damage and it means she can't feel anything in her legs. Her balance is affected as well.'

'You wouldn't think it watching this,' said Larry.

'I know,' replied Charlie, who had really done her homework. 'That's why I wanted you to see it. Her website says she went to Riding for the Disabled when she was nine years old – her physio had recommended it – and now she's won five gold medals at two Paralympic Games.'

Polly's eyes widened like a kitten spotting a toy. 'That's incredible.' Her voice sounded croaky.

Charlie touched her arm. 'You see? You can still do anything,' she said quietly. 'You might have to do it differently, but it doesn't mean it can't be done.'

Polly bit her bottom lip and stared at the screen. The boys leaped up and headed outside. They'd been sitting down chatting pleasantly for at least twenty minutes, which was a new personal best. It must now be time for a fight.

'Shall we go out and see the horses?' Charlie asked.

Polly nodded. She picked up her crutch, pushed herself from the chair and went out into the farmyard. They discussed dressage movements and how they dated back to the time of the Ancient Greeks, who valued horsemanship as a skill. The Greeks thought it could be useful to have a horse who would rear on command or could spin round in a tiny space and gallop off in the opposite direction. They talked about the Spanish Riding School in Vienna, which had taken the idea of equine performance to a whole new level in the sixteenth century and the *Cadre Noir*, the group of officers in the French cavalry who were famed for their riding ability.

The girls were lost in a world of horsey dreams, sharing their appreciation of skilled riding and their understanding of good training. Since Polly's accident, Charlie had been very careful not to talk about horses too much because she didn't want her friend to feel sad about the thing she had loved and seemed to have lost. This felt new and exciting.

'I think we need to write up a training schedule,' Polly said. 'My physio did one for me but I ripped it up.'

'Why?'

'Because I wasn't hitting the targets on the dates I was meant to and it just made me dep–' Polly broke off mid-word. 'It made me *annoyed*. So I ripped it up into tiny pieces and threw it in the bin.'

Charlie looked at her friend in shock. This didn't sound like the Polly she knew. She realized Polly might be dealing with things she had no idea about. Things that Polly had hidden from her.

They reached the gate to the field. Charlie whistled loudly and watched as Percy raised his head and looked at them. She waved a carrot in the air. That did the trick and Percy started lumbering towards them, Noble Warrior following elegantly behind.

She gave Percy the carrot, which was a little disappointing for him, as he would have preferred a packet of mints, twenty cubes of sugar and a few apples. The only thing he had gone off in the last year or so was bananas, after the kidnappers had used them to poison him when they grabbed Noble Warrior from under his nose.

Charlie put a headcollar on Noble Warrior and led him towards the barn so that she could groom him. Percy followed.

Boris trotted ahead of them, raising one hind leg and hopping along on three legs.

'Is he doing that to make me feel better?' Polly laughed.

'No,' Charlie said. 'He's always done it. I think it's a Border terrier thing. He's not self-conscious about it, that's for sure.'

Polly found she could brush Noble Warrior without her crutch. She used her left hand to balance herself on his body and the other to brush energetically with long smooth strokes. Soon his coat started to gleam and his mane and tail flowed straight and soft.

'He'll feel better already,' said Polly as she stood back to admire her work. 'I know I only started to feel human again when I got home from the hospital and was allowed to have a shower. The relief of being clean all over!'

Charlie held two sets of racing girths in her hands. She buckled one to the other so that they could stretch right round Noble Warrior's tummy. She had wound together more baler twine to make two reins, which she looped through the girth and doubled back to the bit rings on his bridle.

'What are you doing?' Polly asked.

'I'm making draw reins. They'll help keep his head down low so that when we work him he's arching his neck and he's really using his back. I'm not going to do them very tight because I don't want him to feel restricted, but I saw it on a Carl Hester dressage masterclass and I think it'll help Noddy build the muscles he needs in his neck and across his back.'

Charlie led Noble Warrior into the field and over to the home-made arena and started to lunge him round her. Polly had asked Charlie's brothers to drag a couple of straw bales to the edge of the arena so that she could sit comfortably and watch. They had built a big straw sofa with two bales as a back support and one bale at the front to sit on.

'Is that OK?' Larry asked, placing a rug over the straw so that it wasn't so prickly.

'That's great. Thanks so much.' Polly smiled at him. 'Could you do me a big favour?'

'Sure.'

'Could you bring me a pad and a pencil? I need to start working up a schedule so that we can give him a gradual programme over the next six months.'

Larry ran towards the house and was back again within minutes.

'Could you make it a bit sooner than that?' he asked as he thrust the pad at Polly.

'Why?'

'It's just that the supermarket opening is in October and it would really help us if he was looking, you know, a bit more like a horse who might once have been capable of winning the Derby!'

Polly bit her lip. 'You know your sister's really not happy about the supermarket idea.'

'Yeah. I know she won't listen to us. But . . .' He paused. 'She might listen to you . . .'

Charlie was oblivious to everything but the movement of the horse around her. Having walked Noble Warrior for ten minutes in each direction, she decided it was time for a change of gear.

She clicked her tongue to ask him to move forward into trot. He rounded his neck and she could see the power coming through from his back end. Soon he was glistening with sweat as she worked him on both reins.

'That's a good boy.' She kept encouraging him to keep up the energy. 'It's all about power, not pace.'

Finally, she asked him to move forward into canter.

'Wow!' Polly shouted from the edge of the arena. 'Look at him move. He's so well balanced and he looks to have a lovely comfortable motion. I bet he'd feel like a rocking horse to ride.'

Charlie eased Noble Warrior back to a walk and undid the draw reins. She let him lower his head and stretch out, walking in a larger circle so that he could really loosen up. He was blowing with the effort and his skin was dark with sweat.

'That'll do for day two, I think,' she said.

Polly heaved herself up from the straw bales and leaned on her crutch for support. She held her pad in the other hand.

'That's plenty and, to be honest, I wouldn't do more than that until at least week three,' she said. 'I've made a chart here and I reckon you'll have him looking sleek and toned by the end of September.'

Charlie smiled. 'This is fun. I like the idea of having a goal for him and I think he's enjoying it too.' She patted Noddy's warm neck. 'Fancy a lift back? It'll be a bit warm up there, but you've got trousers on so it won't feel too sweaty.'

This time Polly didn't hesitate. She used the

straw sofa she'd been sitting on, climbing on to the top of it to get herself level with the horse's back.

Charlie looked towards the farmhouse to check no one was watching. She could see the boys collecting eggs, and above that she thought she saw a shadow pass across her bedroom window.

'Good boy.' Polly heaved herself into position and patted Noble Warrior's neck. Then Charlie led him away from the dressage arena back towards the stables. She could hear Polly quietly singing to herself.

Suddenly, a loud bang caused the chickens to squawk and scatter. Even Percy lifted his head in surprise and came trotting towards them. Noble Warrior immediately tensed up. His tail lifted into the air and he started to prance.

Polly gasped.

'It's OK, Noddy,' Charlie tried to keep her voice calm, but Noble Warrior's eyes were popping out of his head. 'It was just the tractor dropping something near the milking shed. There we go, it's all OK, no need to panic.'

She glanced back at Polly, who was wincing in pain.

'I can't keep myself in the middle of his back!' There was desperation in her voice.

Charlie tried to grab her leg to help her stay in position, but it was too late. Polly started sliding to the right. She didn't have the power in her left side to keep herself up. Charlie switched sides, but wasn't in time – and as Polly fell into a crumpled heap, Noble Warrior stopped prancing. He stood still and looked round at her.

Charlie helped Polly to her feet, her heart thumping.

'Are you OK?'

'I feel such an idiot. That all happened in slow motion and I couldn't do anything to stop it. It's just so *stupid*.' Polly hit her left leg with her right hand. 'It's all your fault. Useless leg. *Useless!*'

Charlie put a comforting arm round her shoulder. 'I know. I know how you feel.'

Polly glared at her. 'How? How do you know? You have *no idea*!'

She sat down again and hit the ground. Noble Warrior took two steps backwards and placed his head in Polly's lap. He nudged her gently in the chest, forcing her to look at him.

Charlie knew that Noble Warrior was a sensitive soul and he would never intentionally hurt anyone. He only behaved badly when he was scared.

'I suppose you're trying to tell me to get back on, aren't you?' Polly said to the horse.

Charlie said nothing and watched as Noddy nudged her again, very gently. She could see her friend silently mouthing numbers. She was counting to ten.

'OK. You win. Charlie, will you help me back on him?'

'Are you girls all right?' Charlie heard her mother's voice calling to them.

'Quick!' she said. 'Let's get you up on your feet. Here, lean on him for support.'

She helped Polly to her feet and encouraged her to rest on Noddy's shoulder.

'Yes, Mum, we're fine,' Charlie called back.

Caroline Bass appeared, walking purposefully towards them. Charlie hoped she hadn't seen what had just happened.

'I was just checking Noddy didn't get scared. Dad was unloading the extra feed for the cows and he made a right racket. Was he OK?'

'Yes, Mrs Bass, he was fine,' Polly answered quickly. 'He's so much less jumpy these days. I really think he's grown up.'

'Hmm. Has he?' Mrs Bass looked at both of the girls and at the horse between them, and raised her left eyebrow. 'Are you sure it's wise to be walking without your crutch, Polly?'

Charlie bit her lip. Her mother always seemed to know when something was up.

'Oh, silly me, I left it by the arena,' Polly replied calmly. 'I was leaning against Noddy instead. He's far better than a crutch!'

'Were you indeed? Well, you just be careful because if I return you to your mother in a worse state than she brought you in, I don't think she'll be letting you come and stay again.'

Polly laughed lightly. 'Oh, Mrs Bass, don't you worry. I'm getting stronger every day.'

'Well, that's very good to hear. Now why don't you and Charlie make your way steadily back to the stables and I'll just grab your crutch and meet you there.'

'Thanks, Mum,' said Charlie.

Mr Williams came to pick up his daughter the next day.

'Hi, Charlie. How's Noble Warrior coming

along?' he asked. 'I hope you're keeping him busy. You can't let racehorses do nothing at all. It's not what they're bred for.'

'Oh, he's great, Mr Williams. Polly and I have devised a training schedule for him. We're using dressage to get him fit and he's really taken to it.' She didn't mention the supermarket. The more she thought about it, the more she cringed at the thought of Noddy prancing up and down the aisles.

Mr Williams smiled at Polly. 'Are you helping out, love? That's great news. It'll do you both the world of good.'

Polly beamed at her father. 'It's helping Noddy out of his depression,' she said. 'It's already making a difference, I think.'

Mr Williams smiled, taking Polly's crutch as she got into the car. Charlie went to the passenger door to talk to her about when she could next come and stay. As they said goodbye, she saw Mr Williams give her mother a small leather bag – probably a present to say thank you.

She waved as the Williamses' car pulled away, already excited about the next time she would see her friend.

Chapter 5

Over the rest of the summer holidays, Polly came to stay at Folly Farm as often as she could. She and Charlie worked on Noble Warrior's paces and his rhythm, and Larry devised a soundtrack that would give him a different beat every few minutes. Every time they finished a training session, Polly clambered on Noddy's back to ride him homewards to the stables.

What with all the training for Noble Warrior,

Charlie found herself feeling fitter and stronger. She was sure she'd had a bit of a growth spurt too – her jodhpurs were coming up short above her ankles, and when she'd gone shopping with her mother for a new pair, Mrs Bass had noticed the change.

'I'll bet you're almost tall enough for the basketball team now!' she said, putting an arm round Charlie's shoulder as they exited the shop.

Charlie rolled her eyes. 'Netball team, Mum!'

'Oh yes, darling,' said her mother. 'I'm thinking of the book I'm editing – it's all about women's sport at the Olympics. Netball's not even an Olympic sport, you know! But I bet you'll be a perfect fit for your school team this term.'

Charlie sighed. Her *mother* might think she was ready, but Flora Walsh, the captain of the first netball team, had overlooked Charlie for the last year. The popular netball girls were hardly going to notice she'd gained a couple of inches and sign her right up. She shook her head. She shouldn't care about that. The most important thing was to focus on her equestrian efforts and get it right for Noble Warrior and Polly.

'How's Noddy's training going, girls?' Mrs Bass asked one evening as they sat round the kitchen table for supper.

'Wonderful, thank you,' replied Polly.

'What have you been up to?' said Mrs Bass with her head on one side.

'Oh, you know. This and that,' Charlie jumped in. 'Getting Noddy fit. Polly's written up a brilliant schedule and it's working. He's starting to look toned and athletic again.'

'That's good news.' Larry winked at Polly. 'You've done that in double-quick time.'

'And what about you, Polly?' Charlie's father asked. 'How are you doing, fitness-wise?'

'We've been working on Polly too, Dad,' said Charlie quickly. 'Her movement and her strength are so much better, aren't they, Pol?' Charlie noticed that her mother had raised an eyebrow.

'Sure are. I'm a medical miracle!' Polly said.

'And what do you think has been the key to that?' Charlie's mother asked slowly.

'Extreme Pilates,' said Polly firmly.

'That's what you call it, is it?' Mrs Bass looked from Charlie to Polly and back again, her eyebrow still hovering towards her hairline. 'Well, just be careful. I wouldn't want Polly's mother to get the wrong idea and stop her from coming to stay.'

'Understood!' said Charlie.

The girls left the table and disappeared to the sitting room. Someone had set up YouTube on the TV and there was a documentary ready to watch. It was about disabled horse riders, and on the screen as they entered the room was a man who had lost two limbs after being struck by lightning.

'This is amazing,' Polly said. 'He's perfectly balanced with one arm and leg.' She watched him cross the diagonal of the dressage arena in extended trot and shook her head in disbelief. 'Incredible. I wish I could do that.'

They looked at the adjusted tack some of the riders used. One had a loop at the front of the saddle so that she could grip with her hand if she needed extra support. Another had thick knee rolls to help keep the legs in place and a higher cantle to add support to the back.

They watched an American rider who was a double-leg amputee. With two long whips in her hands, she had trained her horse to respond to tiny flicks as it would have done to a squeeze from the lower leg. She had straps across the top of the saddle passing over the top of her thighs to keep her in position.

'Her upper-body strength is epic. Look how secure she is in the saddle.' Charlie pointed at the screen.

'I wonder what exercise routines they follow to make them that strong?' Polly said.

'Cup of tea, girls?' Mrs Bass came in carrying two mugs. 'Thought you'd find that interesting.' She nodded at the screen as she put down the mugs.

Charlie frowned and wondered what her mother was up to. She had been thinking about how to encourage Polly without pushing her too far. She knew that she had to get the right balance between showing her how much others had achieved without making her feel insecure about her own progress. She needed Polly to feel more confident when they went back to school and not to worry so much about being judged.

Mrs Bass smiled at the two girls.

'Anything is possible,' she said as she left the room, leaving Charlie wondering.

Charlie turned back to Polly. 'I think we need to invent a new word,' Charlie said. 'Diffability.'

'What?'

'*Diffabilty*. You're not disabled, disadvantaged or disappointed. You're not *dis*-anything. You're *different*. And that means we have to find different ways to do the things you want to do. You've been getting stronger and braver every time you've got on Noddy and I genuinely think he knows how to look after you.'

'I know he does. And I love riding him.' Polly looked out of the window as she spoke. 'Even if it's only to walk home to the stables. I watch him learning how to do dressage and I wish it was me on his back. I'd love that more than anything.'

'Joe always said you'd make a great team,' Charlie said craftily.

Polly didn't answer, but Charlie saw something like regret in her eyes. Eventually she spoke. 'I'd make a fool of myself. If he got spooked by anything at all, I know I haven't got the strength to hold myself in the saddle. If he bolted I wouldn't be able to stop him, and how on earth would I convince my parents to let me even try? They'll barely allow me out of the front door.'

'We'll deal with that when we have to. I've been looking for an instructor,' Charlie announced. She pulled up a new screen on the TV and started typing in the search bar. 'And I think this person could work for you and Noddy. She's called Cecilia Cameron and it says here she has "over thirty years' experience of teaching adults and children with a range of different requirements". Look, she's got an official endorsement from Riding for the Disabled.'

Polly glanced at the screen and looked away again.

'We can call it Riding for the *Diffabled*, if you like?' Charlie suggested.

'That's not the issue,' Polly said. 'It's just not going to happen. I mean, how would we get there without telling your parents? If we tell them, they'll tell mine, and that will be the end of that.' She sighed. 'Anyway, Noddy is happiest here. If we took him somewhere else, he might panic.'

Charlie knew that it was more likely that Polly herself was insecure about riding in front of strangers.

'I think Noddy is braver than we give him credit for,' Charlie said gently. 'I think he will be surprised when he gets there at how much he will enjoy being in front of other people. Miss Cameron is very good. She's coached people to Paralympic gold medals and all sorts.'

She stopped talking and left a gap for Polly to respond. When her friend said nothing, Charlie continued. 'There's a slot on Wednesday evenings we could get in.'

'My mother is busy on Wednesdays,' Polly said.

'Perfect.' Charlie dug Polly in the ribs. 'We can get you a few lessons and then, by the time she sees you riding, you'll be doing a full dressage test!'

Polly bit her lip and stared out of the window. The sky was darkening and tiny drops of rain appeared on the pane.

'Hey, look!' she shouted, heaving herself off the sofa and moving towards the door. 'It's raining. It's finally raining!'

The two girls rushed outside to feel the raindrops falling on their hands. They looked at the sky and Charlie grasped Polly's arms. They leaned backwards, away from each other, so that their

faces were turned upwards as they let the rain splash on to their cheeks.

'Rain, rain, beautiful rain!' sang Charlie, tasting the drops on her tongue. 'This must be a sign.'

She pulled Polly to an upright position and locked her in a solid stare.

'The summer is nearly over, and we'll be back at school next week. You have to see Cecilia Cameron, even if it's only for an assessment. Please say you will. Please, Polly.'

She squeezed Polly's hands and tried to transmit courage and strength through her fingertips.

'OK, OK!' said Polly, grinning. 'Anything to stop the death stare! I'll go. In return, I think you should properly get behind the supermarket idea. Larry's been working really hard on that blog – he's taken before and after photos, he's made a film as well, and I think he and Harry really believe it would be good.'

'Good for Noddy or good for them?'

'Good for Noddy . . .' She paused. 'But maybe good for others as well. It's a really strong message, honestly it is. You should ask them more about it. It's not like an ordinary supermarket.'

Charlie considered. 'OK. Here's the deal. If you have a lesson with Miss Cameron, I'll let Harry and Larry tell me all about the magic supermarket.'

'Deal!' said Polly. 'But how are we going to manage the lesson without telling our parents?'

'Don't worry,' replied Charlie. 'Leave that bit to me.'

Chapter 6

Charlie wasn't looking forward to the first day back at school. She had so enjoyed the summer holidays, being free to work with Noble Warrior and spending time with Polly, watching both of them get stronger. She played with Boris as she followed her brothers down the drive. Boris tried to bite the laces on her shoes and she tried to hop out of the way, laughing as he barked, ran backwards and succeeded in getting a mouthful of laces. He shook his head from side to side with a low, playful growl. She lifted up her foot and he hung on, swinging from side to side.

'Boris, leave!' she commanded as they reached the end of the drive. He looked up at her to check she was serious. *'Leave it!'*

After a pause he released his grip and let go of her foot. He wagged his tail and she leaned down to scratch his head. 'You are the daftest dog in the world!'

The school bus pulled up bang on time and Harry and Larry bounced on board, high-fiving their friends and running to the back row. Charlie clambered up the steps slowly, turning to wave goodbye to Boris and make sure he trotted back down the drive to the farmhouse.

'All right, my love?' said Mrs Wheeler the bus driver kindly. 'It'll never be as bad as you think it is. Come on, let's turn that frown upside down!'

Charlie shrugged and said nothing. She took the seat behind her.

'How was your summer, Mrs Wheeler?'

'It was very nice, thank you, Charlie,' the bus driver replied as she indicated and pulled away. 'How lovely of you to ask. And I expect you got up to all sorts of fun and games with those animals, didn't you?'

They chatted all the way to school, which helped Charlie forget her nerves. She always hated the first day of term and she knew that she had to steel herself to help protect Polly.

'Thanks, Mrs Wheeler,' she said as she jumped down from the bus. 'I really appreciate – you know . . .'

'Any time, my love.'

Charlie popped her head back through the door to ask a question.

'Just one more thing, Mrs Wheeler.' Charlie had had an idea. 'Can you drive a horsebox?'

Mrs Wheeler thought for a second.

'I s'pose so,' she said. 'Same as a bus, really, but with horses rather than fighting kids in the back. Should be easier, to be honest. Why do you ask, my love?'

'Oh, it's nothing, just good to know our options. Thanks so much, Mrs Wheeler.'

Charlie smiled as she walked towards the school entrance. She spotted Mrs Williams opening the car door for Polly and made a beeline for her so that they could walk in together.

'Hey! Charlie! Hang on!'

She was stopped in her tracks by a group of girls, all of them tall and athletic. They were everything Charlie *wanted* to be – fit, confident, self-assured and cheerful.

'You've grown over the summer,' said Helen Danson. She was the goal attack in the school netball team.

'Have I?' Charlie lifted her chin and smiled.

'Definitely,' Helen responded.

Flora Walsh flicked back her long blonde ponytail and looked Charlie up and down. She was the first-team captain, tall and graceful as a gazelle. All the boys walking by looked at her and Charlie noticed one of them staring so hard that he walked straight into an electric car-charging post. Flora had that effect.

'Wanna come and train with us this afternoon?' she asked casually.

Charlie's mouth fell open. She couldn't believe it. 'Oh my gosh, yes! I'd love to.'

'Wicked. See you at three.' Flora walked off, cool as anything – unaware that she had just transformed Charlie's vision of the term ahead.

'Let's find out what she's made of,' Helen Danson whispered to Flora as they walked away, both flicking their ponytails from side to side.

Charlie looked round to find Polly, eager to tell her the news. She caught sight of Mrs Williams's brake lights as the car made its way out of the school car park. She swivelled round and scanned the playground, looking for Polly again. Nothing.

Charlie ran towards the swing doors and hurled herself through them. She stopped in the reception area, looking around. She listened. She heard screams of girls greeting each other after weeks apart, noises coming from iPhones as people played each other videos from their holidays, and faintly,

in the distance, she could hear a clicking noise. She *knew* that sound. She ran towards it and finally she saw Polly, her crutch clicking on the hard school floor with every stride. Charlie paused, eyes widening as she watched the other students moving out of Polly's way without even looking at or speaking to her. They were all staring at the crutch.

Charlie walked quickly to catch up with her best friend and tried not to listen to the snippets of conversation reverberating around them.

'Not allowed out of the house.'

'Apparently, she can't do *any* sport . . .'

'Pol! Wait for me!' Charlie shouted, her face suddenly flushed with fury. She stared at Nadia, the girl who'd made the comment about Polly not being able to do sport. Charlie knew she was in the netball team already. She had been their most important defender last year, always blocking the opposition, but getting into plenty of trouble with referees for fouls. She was talking to the boy next to her with relish, as if she actually enjoyed imparting this gossip about Polly.

'She's talking rubbish,' Charlie said loudly as she walked past them. 'Nasty Nadia loves to spread gossip, even when it's totally invented.' She caught up with her friend. 'Polly! I was going to walk in with you. Why didn't you wait?'

Polly marched on, her crutch clicking on the floor like a metronome. She didn't answer.

Charlie tugged at her sleeve and made her stop. 'Polly, what is it? What did I do? I'm sorry I got distracted, but I ran after you as soon as I could.'

'*Ran* after me? Lucky you!' Polly's eyes glistened. 'Lucky you to be able to do that. To be fast enough and tall enough and sporty enough that the netball girls finally notice you. That's what you really want, isn't it? To be in their gang.'

Charlie shook her head in disbelief. 'I'm made up that they asked me, that's for sure! But it's not about being in a *gang*, Polly. They're not exactly going to replace you as my friend. That's not how it works!'

'Isn't it?' Polly spat. 'I think it's exactly how it works. Why would you want to be with me when you can hang out with the cool, sporty, beautiful girls? I can hear what they say as I walk by. I see the look in their eyes. They think I'm a freak. Why would you want to be friends with a freak, Charlie? Why?'

Charlie was completely thrown. She had spent so much time with Polly this summer, had seen her flourish and grow in confidence as well as physical strength. Where had all this anger come from? What had happened between the car park and the corridor that had put their friendship at risk?

'You're *not* a freak. You're my friend and you will be until the day I die! I'm sorry I wasn't there for you. I wanted to be at your side when you came in.'

'Why? To protect me – is that what you think? Are you my great defender? The heroine of my story? Do I need Charlie Bass by my side every minute of the day if I'm going to get through school?'

Polly turned and walked on towards their classroom, her crutch hitting the floor with added force.

Charlie stood and stared after her. She felt as if she had been slapped hard on the cheek. She looked behind and saw Nadia smirking. Nadia licked her finger, raising it into the air and striking it downwards, as if chalking up a scoreline of 1–0.

Feeling sick, Charlie followed her friend into the classroom at a distance. When she entered the room she saw there was no space to sit next to Polly as she usually did. Instead, she had to sit two rows behind her. She was in utter conflict. She wanted so much to be on the netball team, but she didn't want to desert Polly. Why did it feel as if she had to choose?

She couldn't concentrate on the lesson at all. Dr Patterson was banging on about evolution and how the human brain was always changing. Something about mobile phones and social media. Blah blah. None of it mattered to Charlie. All *her* brain was concerned about was her friendship with Polly. How could she fix it? She didn't want to pull out of netball training. She'd been waiting a whole year to get the chance to be in the same room as the first team and she didn't think it was fair of Polly to expect her to ditch that dream. There *had* to be another solution.

'Coding is the key.' Dr Patterson was wittering on about computer programming and how not enough girls were interested. 'There are loads of apprenticeships out there, but it seems that most girls don't believe they have the capability to write code. Look back at history, however, and it will tell you that the great technology breakthroughs were made by women. Back in the nineteenth century, Ada Lovelace designed the first algorithm for a computer. In the nineteen sixties, Grace Hopper designed a compiler – or translator – for the language of programming. Women were often employed *as* computers, and then when computers were introduced at places like NASA, it was women who worked out how to use them.'

Charlie saw Polly put up her hand.

'Yes, Polly?'

'Dr Patterson, if women in the nineteenth and twentieth centuries weren't afraid of computers, why are so few twenty-first-century women developing new programmes to solve modern problems?'

Dr Patterson pushed her glasses up her nose and inhaled. 'I have often wondered about that and I believe it comes down to two things – gender stereotyping and confidence.'

She paused and looked around the room at the boys and girls in their uniforms, sitting behind desks in front of her. Her eyes came to rest again on Polly.

'We are conditioned to behave in the way we think befits our gender,' she explained. 'Social media, which I explained earlier can cleverly convince your brain to buy certain products, can also train you to behave in a certain way. Girls, for example, are told they should wear as many different clothes as they can, but if they dare to have a different hairstyle from everyone else ...'

Dr Patterson gazed around the room again. Charlie could see girls tossing their ponytails from side to side. She ran her hand through her own short hair and shrank into her seat.

'As Billie-Jean King, the pioneer of professional women's tennis, has said – boys are taught to be strong and powerful, girls are taught to be pretty and perfect.'

Charlie started taking notes in her exercise book. She wrote down 'pretty' and 'perfect' and then drew a line through them. Dr Patterson was warming to her theme now and continued to hold court.

'Many philosophers far wiser than me will tell you how damaging it is to humanity to expect any one set of people to behave in a regimented and uniform way. It limits their capacity to create and it leads to intolerance. If anyone dares to be different, they are perceived as being weaker and will be cast out from the group.'

Charlie was scribbling hard in her book. This was interesting. She saw Polly put her hand up again.

'And what, miss, should you do if you can't help being different? How do you make sure you're not the one who is cast out of the group?'

'Good question, Polly,' Dr Patterson replied. She pushed her glasses up her nose again. 'I don't have all the answers, but the one thing I would say is, *Don't adapt to fit in.* I truly believe we should celebrate difference. If we're all going to be exactly the same, we might as well be sheep and *baa* at each other, rather than speak!' A few people giggled. 'You can always make yourself useful by being different. Every group needs people with a variety of skills. Every team needs support staff as well as their star striker.'

Charlie saw Polly nodding and noticed that she too was writing.

When the bell rang for the end of class, Charlie waited. She knew that all the other pupils would get up as fast as they could and run for the door. Dr Patterson's lesson had made everyone – boy or girl – feel self-conscious. But Polly couldn't move that quickly and it was safer for her to wait until the rush had ebbed away.

Charlie moved to her side. 'That was interesting, wasn't it?' she said, trying to sound nonchalant.

'Yeah.'

'I wrote down lots of notes.'

'Me too,' Polly said, packing her books into her bag and avoiding Charlie's eye.

'Polly – I . . .' Charlie steeled herself. It was worth a shot. 'I wondered if you'd be interested in . . . giving advice?' Polly looked at her, eyes narrow. 'To me, to help me make it on to the netball team? Like you do with Noddy.'

'What sort of advice?' Polly asked.

'Everything, really. I'm scared. I don't know if I'm good enough and I certainly don't know if I can fit in. I don't like Nadia, for one thing, and I don't think I want to be on a team with girls like her.'

Polly didn't reply.

'You know that schedule you drew up for Noddy?' Charlie said. 'It was really useful and it's helped us plan a steady programme for him so that he's got much stronger over the summer. He's also way more confident, not spooking at every noise or shadow. It would be a bit like that, but with . . . more . . .'

Charlie smiled at Polly, trying to encourage the character she knew and loved to show her face again.

Finally Polly spoke. 'I guess it might be helpful to have someone watching from the sidelines, analysing training and that sort of thing.' Charlie spotted a gleam in her eye and had to stop herself throwing her arms round her friend. 'I could even build a programme on the computer to break down the numbers,' Polly went on. 'Work out whether there's something simple you can do that would make you invaluable to the team or whether it's more complicated than that.'

'Coursework for Doctor Patterson!' Charlie joked. 'Oh, and by the way,' she added, 'I've got an idea for how we get Noddy to your lesson without our parents knowing.'

'Oh?' Polly said.

'Mrs Wheeler can drive the horsebox.'

'Mrs Wheeler?'

'She drives the school bus,' Charlie explained. 'She reckons driving a horsebox would be much easier – and she's sound. She wouldn't rat on us.'

They walked out of the classroom together and Charlie felt her heart rate returning to normal for the first time since their argument in the corridor. She put a hand out, silently offering to carry Polly's bag.

'Thanks,' said Polly gratefully.

That afternoon, Charlie joined the first team for netball practice, taken by Mrs Kennedy, who was also the headmistress. Polly came along to watch, sitting on a bench at the side of the indoor sports hall.

'Hey, Polly!' Mrs Kennedy called out. 'Good to have you with us.'

'What's she doing here?' Nadia hissed at Charlie as she barged past her. 'She can't play netball!'

'Give her a break,' said Flora Walsh. 'She's not causing any trouble.'

Charlie said nothing and tried to concentrate on the training drills. There were plastic markers on the floor of the wooden court. The girls each had to sprint from the wall to the second marker, about ten metres away, jump as high as they could, then run sideways for four steps and back for four,

then turn and sprint to the wall again.

'That's it, Charlie! Keep those knees nice and bouncy,' shouted Mrs Kennedy.

Every time Charlie turned to go back to her starting position, Nadia was there, blocking her path. She either had to swerve abruptly or crash into her.

'Watch out, clumsy! Can't you see where you're going?' Nadia shouted loudly enough for Mrs Kennedy and the rest of the team to hear.

'You've got to keep your wits about you,' Helen Danson said to Charlie as they gathered to do the next drill. 'Always be aware of where the other players are.'

'But it's not my fault!' Charlie tried to argue.

'Doesn't matter.' Helen wasn't interested in excuses. 'You'll be the one to get penalized on the court if you run into the opposition. Nadia's only trying to help you.'

Charlie shook her head. It felt so unfair.

Mrs Kennedy placed a ladder on the floor and asked Flora Walsh to demonstrate the next drill.

Flora smoothed down her skirt and glided forward. She hopped from one foot to the next, together then apart, running from one ladder square to the next without touching the bars. She was moving so fast that Charlie only saw a blur of dancing feet.

'So, first foot into the space, second foot in and then take off again into the next space. Got it?' said Mrs Kennedy, taking a watch out of her pocket. 'Fast as you can.'

Charlie glanced over to Polly with fear in her eyes. Polly nodded her encouragement and gestured with her hands as if suggesting a trotting movement. *That's it*, thought Charlie. *It's like Noble Warrior learning to lift his knees in trot.*

Mrs Kennedy blew her whistle and timed every girl in the ladder drill. They had seconds added if they hit the ladder bars. Flora Walsh went first and sprinted over the ladder, touched the wall at the far end and came back even faster, not even close to touching the rungs. Helen Danson went next and, although she was quick, she hit at least two bars.

'Right, Charlie. Your turn,' said Mrs Kennedy.

Charlie stood rooted to the spot. She couldn't move forward or back. She was frozen.

'Come on, we haven't got all day,' snarled Nadia behind her.

'Told you she didn't have the bottle,' Helen Danson said to Flora.

Charlie heard Mrs Kennedy blow her whistle, but still she couldn't move.

'They're off!' she heard Polly shout from the sidelines, and somehow that triggered a thought in her head. She had a flashback to Derby Day when the stalls opened and she knew she had to ride Percy for all she was worth across the middle of Epsom Racecourse to the winning post to get there before Noble Warrior.

'Kick on!' Polly shouted again.

Charlie took off and ran as fast as she could, her feet landing in the first ladder box together and then springing into the next. She finished the first section cleanly, ran to the wall to touch it and sprint back. As she came back along the ladder she looked up with two sections to go. Nadia was standing way too close to the last box. She was going to crash into her. She hesitated for a split second and lost her concentration. Charlie's foot caught the second last bar and she went tumbling to the floor.

Mrs Kennedy rushed over.

'Are you all right, Charlie? That was a nasty fall. Such a shame, as you were really flying there.'

Charlie sat up, dazed and embarrassed. Her knee was throbbing and she felt dizzy.

'I'm fine,' she said. 'Honestly, right as rain. Just a silly mistake. I took my eyes off where I was putting my feet. Stupid, really.'

She gritted her teeth and pushed herself to her feet, trying to disguise the pain in her knee. Nadia smiled thinly at her and offered an arm for support.

'No, thanks, I'm fine.' Charlie waved her away.

She saw Flora looking concerned and overheard Helen saying, 'Are you sure she's up to this? It's not fair if she's not ready.'

Charlie smiled as brightly as she could and tried to ignore the throbbing pain in her knee.

'Nadia, you're next,' said Mrs Kennedy. 'And Charlie, why don't you go and sit on the bench with Polly for a few minutes.'

'You can compare notes,' Nadia snarled as Charlie held her head high and tried not to limp. She flopped down on to the bench next to Polly.

'Hard work?' asked Polly.

'I've never tried so hard in my life. Now I know what Noddy must feel like!'

Charlie rubbed her knee, which was already red and swollen. They watched Nadia complete the ladder challenge, nowhere near as fast as Charlie, but without mistakes or a fall.

Polly rubbed her friend on the back to comfort her.

'I think you probably know how I feel as well,' she said. 'It's not much fun when you can't join in.'

In the meantime, at Mrs Kennedy's request, one of the players had brought some ice for Charlie's knee. As she sat there nursing her injury, the pain gradually started to subside.

'What are you thinking?' asked Polly, who was taking notes on the remainder of the training session.

'I'm wondering how you get over it,' Charlie replied.

'You don't,' said Polly. 'You just get *on* with it. That's the key. Just grin and get on with it.'

The training session ended and the netball team dispersed. Mrs Kennedy came to check on Charlie's knee.

'That's a relief. The swelling's coming down already. I don't think you'll have done any serious damage, but if it's still sore tomorrow, make sure you see the nurse.'

Flora waved at Polly and Charlie as the team left the court. 'Come again if you fancy it, Polly. We could do with all the support we can get!'

'See?' Charlie said to her friend. 'They want you back more than me, and they don't even know that you've been taking notes.'

Polly crossed her hands protectively over her notebook. Charlie put her right hand gently on top.

'Come on. Show me. I know how good you are at seeing what others can't.'

Polly opened her notepad for Charlie to look at. She had written five headings with notes scribbled under each.

Movement

Communication

Anticipation

Concentration

Confidence

'You've got to show this to Flora,' Charlie begged her.

'I can't do that!' Polly snapped the notebook shut.

'Why not?'

'She thinks I'm just a supporter. A cheerleader who can't actually do any cheerleading!' Polly smiled grimly at her own joke.

'She doesn't know what I know,' Charlie said, determined that Polly's talents shouldn't go to waste.

Chapter 7

When Mrs Williams dropped Polly off at Folly Farm on the following Saturday, she stopped for a chat in the kitchen. Charlie and Polly paused by the door to listen.

'Honestly,' Mrs Williams told Mrs Bass, 'I don't know how your Charlie is doing it, but I hear they've developed a new exercise for Polly's posture and I have to say it's working wonders!'

'Well, yes, the thing is, I should probably tell you –'

Charlie pushed through the door before she could finish. 'Mrs Williams,' she said quickly, 'have you heard that Polly came to watch netball training?'

'Did she now?' Mrs Williams raised her eyebrows and smiled. 'That might explain why she was on the computer last night reading about how the England netball team won the Commonwealth gold medal in Australia! She's very taken with the idea of

118

"funetherness" – whatever that means!'

'It's a combination of fun and togetherness,' Polly explained as she followed her friend into the kitchen. 'It's the mantra of England Netball.'

'Well! That sounds excellent.' Mrs Williams looked down to see Boris banging his tail on the floor in support. 'How's your knee, by the way? Polly told me you had a nasty fall in training.'

'Did you?' Mrs Bass looked surprised.

'Oh, yeah,' Charlie replied. 'It was nothing. It's fine now.'

'You're a tough one, you are,' said Mrs Williams. 'I was just telling your mother how much Polly's fitness is improving – isn't it, sweetheart? You're definitely getting stronger. I hope this term at school will be a bit easier.' Mrs Williams smiled, mainly at Boris, and shrugged her shoulders. 'One day at a time, I guess.'

Charlie realized that every time she had seen Polly's mother over the last year, her face had been locked in tension. Now it seemed a tiny bit more relaxed.

'Would it be all right if Polly kept coming here at weekends?' Mrs Williams directed her question at both Charlie and Mrs Bass. Polly nodded vigorously. 'She's always so upbeat when I collect her and I think it's doing her the world of good. Alex is busy at the races on Saturdays and Sundays and he's particularly keen that she should have time away from the racehorses.'

'Obviously Noble Warrior is a racehorse,' said Charlie's mother, 'and you should know that –'

Polly jumped in. 'Ah, but he's a *retired* racehorse and he's completely different now he's not being trained to gallop flat out. We've been teaching him dressage and it's great for his muscle development,' she went on breathlessly.

'As for Polly,' Charlie added, we're working hard on her core strength, Mrs Williams, and we wondered if it would be OK if we went to see an instructor who specializes in working with people recovering from injury and living with a diffability?'

Charlie glanced briefly at her mother, whose left eyebrow had shot towards the ceiling.

120

'A *diffability*?' said Mrs Williams. 'Is that from the same dictionary as *funetherness*?'

'It could be!' said Charlie. 'It just means that you have to approach life differently. This instructor isn't far away and she encourages all sorts of exercise and alternative therapy,' she continued, eager for a reply.

Mrs Williams looked at Polly, who gave her a thumbs up.

'There's a session free on Wednesday,' Polly said. 'That way I can go straight from school.'

Charlie's mother pursed her lips but said nothing.

'Oh, Wednesday evenings are no good, I'm afraid.' Mrs Williams was looking at the diary on her mobile phone. 'I won't be around to do the lifts.'

'That's not a problem,' Charlie said quickly. 'Mrs Wheeler has said she can take us.'

Caroline Bass looked at her daughter with her eyebrow still raised. 'Has she?'

'Yes,' Charlie said firmly. 'We've done all the research, Mum, and it's a fabulous place. Miss Cameron has got all the right endorsements.

Honestly, it will be brilliant.'

'Also, it means I can still work on my fitness while I help out the netball team with theirs,' Polly added.

Mrs Bass looked from Charlie to Mrs Williams, who was smiling broadly.

'She's such a star, young Charlie, and they make such a good team. They're real planners and they've got a solution for everything, haven't they?' Mrs Williams laughed, perhaps a little nervously. '*Diffability*.' She rolled the word around on her tongue as if trying it for size. 'Diffability. I like it.'

She enveloped Charlie in a hug and whispered, 'Thank you,' into the top of her head.

Charlie was thrilled. She needed Mrs Williams to have complete trust in her. Polly gave Charlie a high five as they turned together to head out of the kitchen.

'Charlie does have a good track record of building up confidence,' said Mrs Bass. 'But I think it's a bit different with a person rather than a horse!'

'Oh, I don't know.' Mrs Williams put her phone

back into her bag. 'I think people can sometimes be more straightforward. At least they can tell you how they feel and have a proper discussion!'

'Indeed,' said Mrs Bass, glancing back at Charlie. 'As long as they tell you the truth.'

Charlie gave her mother a grin as she and Polly headed for the stairs. They threw themselves on to the bed to discuss the details.

'We have to go for an assessment and then Miss Cameron will decide whether to take you on,' Charlie said. 'I'll talk to Mrs Wheeler about logistics. We're the last drop on the school run so she could leave the bus here and then take us in the horsebox with Noddy and Percy.'

'How on earth is that going to work?' asked Polly. 'Your dad may have eyes only for the cows but I think even he might notice a big bus parked in his farmyard.'

The girls heard the sound of a departing car as Polly's mother headed home. They were still trying to work out how they could get Noble Warrior and Percy out of the yard, into the horsebox and away for the lesson, when they heard footsteps on the stairs. Charlie stopped talking and Polly's eyes widened at the firm knock on the door.

'May I come in?' Mrs Bass asked politely.

'Sure thing, Mum,' Charlie answered breezily. 'We were just discussing netball drills and how to improve my footwork.'

'Were you?' Mrs Bass was not smiling. 'I wondered if you two wanted to discuss anything with *me*?'

Charlie looked at the floor. 'Don't think so,' she mumbled.

'Really?' Mrs Bass answered. 'Well, good luck with that lesson on Wednesday.'

Charlie chewed the inside of her right cheek. Polly blushed. Mrs Bass waited. Neither of the girls said a word.

Mrs Bass held up her hand.

'I'll tell you what. Why don't you two have a think about it, chat it through with each other and maybe this evening after your dressage training and your ride back to the stables, you might want to

have a full and frank discussion about . . .
everything.'

Mrs Bass turned on her heel and walked out of
the room, closing the door behind her. Polly's eyes
were as wide as saucers. Charlie blew out a deep
breath.

'She knows!' Polly said slowly.

Charlie swallowed hard. Her mother always had
a knack of knowing what she was up to, what she
was thinking and planning. But if she knew, why
hadn't she stopped them?

Charlie thought about the new security camera
on the side of the chicken shed and the reflected
light she kept seeing when she looked up at the
house. Maybe her mother had been on to them for
a while.

'Tell you what, let's find out.' Charlie got off the
bed and walked to her window. It had been raining
on and off since they'd gone back to school, but
today was blessedly a bright, warm day. The leaves
were just starting to turn from their summer green
to the autumn shades of burgundy and ruby, and in

a few weeks, they would start falling from the trees.

Charlie had noticed a ring-shaped mark on the window ledge a few days before, but couldn't work out where it had come from. Maybe she'd left a cup of tea there and it had made a stain. Now, Charlie went to her dressing table and took out some talcum powder.

'What are you doing?' Polly asked.

Charlie took the container of talc and tapped it lightly, showering the window ledge with a very thin layer of white powder.

'We'll see if this is disturbed when we come back.' She noticed Polly's confused expression and grinned. 'Trust me!'

Chapter 8

The girls headed out to the stables to groom Noble Warrior and take him for his lunging session.

'How long this week?' Charlie asked.

Polly consulted her notebook. 'We did forty minutes last weekend so I think forty-five should be fine. I've got a memo here that he's stiffer when he's going right-handed so we need to work on that, and try to improve his flexibility.'

Charlie led Noddy out to the middle of the arena where weeks of hoofprints had left clear tracks marking a circle round the central area. She glanced up at the farmhouse and saw the now-familiar twinkle from her bedroom as the sunlight reflected off something shiny. She wondered if her theory was right.

When they had finished their session in the dressage arena, Charlie noticed a wooden block that had appeared by the side of the arena. It was exactly the right height for Polly to stand on and mount Noble Warrior. Charlie glanced back at the farmhouse and saw a shape move across her bedroom window, just as it had on the first day Polly had ridden Noddy.

'Shall we take the long way home?' she asked.

'Sure.'

They walked along the side of the field, up to the top of the hill and under the trees. Percy realized something was happening without him so he trotted to catch up. Charlie kept a light contact on the leading rein so that she was there in case of

emergency, but in fact it meant that Polly had control of steering Noddy.

'I wish I could ride properly again,' Polly said.

'Oh, I think Miss Cameron will help us with that,' Charlie assured her. 'Roll on Wednesday!'

When they got back to the farmhouse, Charlie and Polly went straight upstairs. Charlie rushed over to the window ledge. She saw two rings, clearly marked in the talcum powder. 'Ha!'

'What do you think it is?' Polly asked.

'Come with me.' Charlie led her friend carefully down the stairs to the bottom of the house. But instead of going to the kitchen, she turned them right towards the library. Her mother had an impressive collection of books that she had once kept stacked in piles in this spare room. But after Noble Warrior won the Derby, Charlie had insisted that her mother spend some of the money on bookshelves, and the library had been born.

'This is *so* impressive,' Polly said. Charlie knew she loved this room. 'I bet you can find a book here on any subject you want.'

Charlie pointed out the different sections.

'Fiction's on this side of the room and non-fiction is over there – but then they're also subdivided into sections like sport or politics or religion. There's a really good one about coaching you might like to read.'

Polly moved towards the sports section and started pulling out books.

'Are we looking for clues?'

'Not there, we're not.'

Charlie moved towards the desk where another book lay open. It was the latest proof copy her mother was reading to check for factual mistakes, typos and grammatical errors. Next to the book was a pair of black binoculars. Charlie picked them up and inspected the lenses on the bottom. She traced her finger around the rim of the lens and smelled it. She tasted it as well, just to make sure.

'I thought so,' she said triumphantly.

'What?'

'Lavender talcum powder tastes horrible!'

She handed them to Polly for inspection.

'I've seen these before,' Polly said, taking the heavy black binoculars and turning them to see the thin layer of talcum powder on the bottom rim. 'My dad had a pair just like these that he used to take to the races. He uses a smaller, lighter pair now, but these always used to be over his shoulder.'

She pointed to a metal badge hanging off the leather strap.

'See that? It's his trainer's badge from 2014. These are Dad's binoculars!'

Charlie frowned. She wasn't surprised to discover

that her mother was watching her, but this was a puzzle. What was she doing with Alex Williams's binoculars?

That night Charlie and Polly had the full and frank conversation that her mother had suggested.

'I know we haven't been honest with you,' Charlie explained. 'But that's because we didn't really know that it would become a regular thing.'

'It started by accident,' Polly added. 'It was almost as if Noddy wanted me to ride him and he's been so sweet and understanding.'

'Apart from that time you fell off him,' said Mrs Bass matter-of-factly.

'You saw that?' Charlie was surprised.

'Of course I did. How do you think I got there so quickly? Now don't worry, I'm not going to spill your secret. I'm just glad you decided to tell *someone* what was going on!'

Charlie felt better once they had included her mum in the plan to help Polly ride again. It was a relief not to be inventing stories and she had been worried about involving Mrs Wheeler unwittingly in their scheme to deceive. She finally plucked up the courage to ask the big question.

'Mum, would you be able to take us to Miss Cameron's lesson on Wednesday?'

Mrs Bass raised an eyebrow as she looked at her daughter and then smiled.

'I thought you'd never ask,' she said.

Chapter 9

Cecilia Cameron was whippet-thin. She had a long, straight back and hair scraped into a bun behind her head. She wore dark blue jodhpurs with suede dividing the legs in half and forming an upside-down U shape on her bottom, a pale blue shirt with the top button done up and a tie tucked underneath a blue tank top. She stood in the middle of an outdoor arena and barked instructions at a group of ten riders, all of whom were being led by adults in green sweatshirts with WILMINGTON RDA on the front of them.

'Sit up! Use your legs! Come on, I want more from you. William, concentrate. That's a good boy. Use your Buttdar!'

Miss Cameron paced in a circle, following the riders and their ponies with her stare. Charlie and Polly watched from a distance.

'What on earth is a *Butt-dar*?' Polly asked with a nervous laugh.

'I haven't a clue.' Charlie was starting to feel anxious herself. Maybe this was a bad idea.

'Use the mirrors, Jessica, and you will see that your lower leg is moving all over the place. Hold it still! That's better. Excellent. Head up and upper body steady! Good girl.'

Round the outside of the arena, halfway down the long side and at each of the short sides, were enormous mirrors, positioned so that the riders could see their own reflections and make adjustments accordingly.

'Right, trot on! Now sit tight, all of you. William,

don't hang on to the reins like that. Come on, leaders, run fast enough for your ponies to actually trot. Mrs Scott, I'm afraid that's not good enough. Yes, I know you're not a runner, but honestly, a little jog round the arena won't kill you, and Thomas needs a challenge.'

Mrs Bass came to stand behind the girls.

'Well, at least you're finally going to ride with proper guidance, Polly.'

Charlie winced in mock horror. 'I hope you're not insulting my riding instruction, Mum?'

'Of course not, Charlie. I'm just relieved that Polly can ride in slightly more controlled circumstances at last. I just spoke to one of the parents whose daughter has cerebral palsy. She said she was terrified the first time she brought her to the class and thought she'd never cope, but says she loves it now. And little Jessica –' she pointed at a round-faced girl on a cob with huge feathered feet at the back of the group – 'hasn't stopped smiling since the minute she got here. Her dad told me she loves that pony more than anything in the world.

She always asks to ride him and she stays behind for an hour to muck out and groom. I guess we already know that the connection with the pony is as important as the riding.'

Charlie nodded vigorously in agreement. 'Yes, and Polly's relationship with Noble Warrior is so special.'

They watched in silence as the adults leading the ponies got redder in the face and starting puffing loudly.

'OK! That'll do. And *walk*. Well done, leaders, and well done, riders. Pat your ponies now and say thank you. I'll be coming round to see how well you've groomed them. I expect those stables to be spick and span as well! Spick and span, I say.'

Jessica, the girl on the cob, leaned forward and put both her arms round her pony. Her face turned towards her father and she grinned so broadly that all her teeth showed.

'I love Sparky!' she shouted. The woman leading her patted her leg.

'I know you do, Jessica. He loves you too. Now

let's brush him off, clean your tack and muck out his stable.'

Jessica beamed.

Charlie watched the line of ten ponies make their way back to the stables.

'Polly Williams, I presume?'

The voice they had heard from a distance was suddenly right beside them. Polly jumped in surprise.

'Which one of you is Polly?'

'Uh, um, I am.'

Miss Cameron stretched out her hand.

'Well, I am delighted to make your acquaintance. We will agree a deal. I will give you my maximum effort if you give me yours? Are you up for it?'

Polly nodded, looking a little stunned.

'And you must be her mother?' Miss Cameron turned to Mrs Bass.

'No. No, I'm not, actually. I'm . . . I'm, ooh, what am I?'

'Her kidnapper?' It was hard to tell if Miss Cameron was joking or not.

'Gosh, no! No, certainly not. I, uh, I just, uh . . .'

Charlie spoke up. 'Miss Cameron, this is my mother and Polly is my best friend. We booked the lesson because we'd read about Wilmington RDA on the internet and we thought you might be the best person to help us.'

'And what is your name?'

'Charlie, miss. Charlie Bass.'

Miss Cameron furrowed her brow as if trying to remember something.

'Charlie Bass? Haven't I heard that name somewhere before?'

Polly opened her mouth to speak, but Charlie got there first. 'Oh, it's a common enough name. I'm always getting people who think they've met or seen a Charlie Bass before.'

Charlie didn't want too many questions about Noble Warrior. She was worried that if Miss Cameron realized that he was the same horse who had won the Derby and then been kidnapped, she might not let Polly take her lessons on him.

Miss Cameron put her head on one side and looked Polly up and down.

'She had an accident,' Mrs Bass started to explain. 'She has nerve damage –'

Miss Cameron put up her hand. 'I've already got all the information I need,' she said firmly. 'This is all about what she can do, not about what you might think she can no longer do.'

Charlie was confused. She hadn't sent Miss Cameron any medical documents. Where had she got them from?

'I'll be able to tell as soon as I see you on a horse how much you will be able to achieve, and I suspect it will be far more than you think.'

She ran her hand across her slicked-back hair and Charlie noticed her knobbly fingers. One seemed to be crooked, as if it had once been broken and never properly reset.

Miss Cameron looked at her watch. 'I need to make an inspection. I will meet you in ten minutes in the arena.'

No-nonsense. That's how Charlie mentally

described Cecilia Cameron. She watched the instructor stride purposefully towards the stables and wondered again if she had made the right decision.

'We'd better not hang about,' she said to Polly, and the two of them took extra care to brush out every trace of straw from Noble Warrior's tail and every speck of dust from his coat. Percy was a more difficult case. He had deposited a spectacularly runny poo down the insides of his back legs, which had turned his white socks brown.

Charlie tried as best she could to wash off the offending smudges, but with little effect. She had decided it would be safer all round if she rode Percy alongside Noble Warrior so that he didn't panic. She could also guide him with a leading rein.

Noble Warrior followed Percy and his poo-smudged hind legs into the outdoor arena. Charlie had found an old towel to fling over his back so that Polly could grip a little better. She figured it would be safer and more comfortable than riding completely bareback.

The horses' hooves sank into the oiled sand-and-rubber surface, which was softer and more forgiving than the sun-baked ground they had been using at home. Brightly coloured bits of rubber, recycled from electrical wires, gave the mixture a bit of elasticity – it was the equine equivalent of a sprung floor for ballet or dance classes. Charlie had threaded the orange plaited string through Noble Warrior's bridle so that she could lead him from her position atop Percy.

'OK, Pol?' she asked.

Polly nodded silently.

Percy paused to admire himself in the mirror. How could anyone fail to appreciate the singular beauty of a chubby Palomino pony with four white socks (even if they were a little splashed), a white-blond mane, one blue eye, one brown and a sun-reddened nose?

Noble Warrior had never seen himself in a mirror before and his reaction was rather different. He snorted and backed away from the dark horse he saw looking back at him. His tail lifted and he

pranced on the spot. Polly's eyes widened in fear, but she tried to keep her voice steady.

'It's OK, Noddy. It's only you. Whoa, boy, steady now.'

She gripped as hard as she could with her right leg, but her other side would not react. Noble Warrior retreated from his reflection and pulled back on the lead rein. Charlie tried to hang on to him, but the rope pulling through her hands burned the insides of her palm and she had to let go as Noble Warrior reared.

'Sit tight, Polly!' Mrs Bass called from the outside of the arena. She began to climb through the rails to try to help.

Charlie tried to position Percy in between the terrified horse and his reflection. She was desperate for Polly and Noble Warrior to pass the assessment. But it wasn't enough.

It all happened in a split second. Noble Warrior saw his own hooves flailing in the air and panicked. He reared again. Polly had no chance. She landed heavily on the grey sand. Noble Warrior's eyes were out on stalks and his ears flicked backwards and forwards.

Caroline ran towards Polly to help her up when a stern voice called out, 'Stay right where you are!'

Miss Cameron walked briskly towards them, carrying a large black saddle on her arm. Mrs Bass froze and then backed away to the fence. Noble Warrior looked at Polly, wincing on the ground, and then back at his own reflection.

'Let him work it out,' Miss Cameron said calmly as she put the saddle over the top of the gate.

Noble Warrior walked gingerly towards the mirror and stuck his nose out. The horse he saw stuck its nose towards him. He turned his head to the left. The other horse turned its head to the right. He lowered his head. The other horse did the same.

'Up you get.' Miss Cameron put out an arm to help Polly to her feet, but offered no comfort or words of concern. Once Polly was standing, Miss Cameron walked towards Noble Warrior, approaching him slowly from behind, murmuring under her breath. She gently took the reins and let him reach out with his nose and actually touch the mirrored glass.

'See, it's only a mirror.' She patted his neck firmly. 'Silly boy.'

'He's been through a lot in the last year,' Charlie tried to explain.

'I'm sure he has,' Miss Cameron said in a clipped tone. 'But we will not tolerate behaviour like that, now, will we?' She started to lead him back towards the gate.

'Now, let's get a saddle on you and see if we can give young Polly a chance to show me what she can do.'

Charlie looked at her friend with concern and mouthed, 'Are you OK?'

Polly nodded.

The saddle had raised knee rolls and a high cantle. Miss Cameron adjusted the stirrups to a length that would allow Polly's legs to hang straight with her heels below the saddle flaps.

'Come on, Polly, no time to shilly-shally.'

To the side of the arena was a bright green block of plastic. It was a portable step, so light that Miss Cameron could scoop it up in one hand and drop it on the left side of Noble Warrior's shoulder.

'Let's get you straight back on.'

She directed Polly to the top of the step, which brought her navel level with Noble Warrior's withers.

'Left foot into the stirrup and then over you swing.'

'But I can't –'

'Yes, you can. Come on. Left leg in my hand, into the stirrup and one-two-hup!'

Standing on her right leg and with her left foot tentatively placed in the stirrup, Polly took advantage of a gentle push from behind and swung her leg over Noble Warrior's back. Charlie saw her grimace as she landed inelegantly in the saddle.

'You'll get better at that,' Miss Cameron said. 'Now just make sure those stirrups feel all right. Do you see that loop on the left side of the saddle? That's there for support if you need it, but let's try to use it only in an emergency.'

Charlie moved towards Noble Warrior, but Miss Cameron raised her hand.

'No need for that. I think we'll see what Polly can do on her own, and if she needs leading, I have plenty of people who can help. You can follow her on the pony and do exactly what I tell her to do.'

Polly looked terrified. Charlie wanted to protect her and look after her, but she also remembered what Polly had said to her at school on the first day of term. Some things she needed to do on her own.

Miss Cameron took her position in the middle of the arena and followed Polly with her eyes. Noble Warrior looked round for Percy and reluctantly moved forward, looking behind again to check his companion was following. Charlie gave Percy a kick in his ample belly to keep him a length behind.

'It's quite a challenge to ride a thoroughbred.' Miss Cameron's voice carried to every corner of the arena, even though she wasn't shouting. 'They can be rather sensitive, as you are well aware. That's it – keep your leg on to get him moving past that mirror. He'll get used to it soon enough. Good girl.'

Polly squeezed her legs against his sides and encouraged him to walk forward. Noble Warrior started to relax.

'I don't know how long I can ride for. We've only been doing a couple of minutes every day and only in walk,' Polly said nervously.

'You'll be fine,' Miss Cameron replied. 'It's my job to make sure of that. Now let me see your shoulders drop a bit. You're so tense you look frozen like a statue! That's it. And let's focus on trying to keep him to the edge of the arena. Ride into those corners.'

Charlie saw Polly's body start to loosen up as she concentrated.

'Butt*dar*!' Miss Cameron shouted out. 'Your leg may be numb, but your *bottom* is not! Use the radar in your bottom to feel the change in rhythm. That's it! Excellent.'

For thirty-five minutes, Cecilia Cameron put Noble Warrior and Percy through their paces. Charlie could feel her legs burning with the effort and her bottom was sore. She wondered how Polly was faring, but there was no opportunity to ask.

'Charlie, bring your pony into the middle here with me. Polly, you stay on the left rein and let's see what Noble Warrior looks like in canter.'

'We haven't –'

But Miss Cameron cut off her protest. 'At the next corner, Polly, ask him to move into canter. That's it and –' she clicked her tongue – '*canter!*'

Noble Warrior responded to the voice command, as he had learned on the lunge rein, leading on the left leg and moving smoothly into canter. Polly's brow furrowed in concentration. She sat into the saddle and tried to keep her left leg from moving. She kept a steady contact with his mouth, and his head dropped a little lower, his neck rounding into an elegant shape.

'Try to turn his head a little more to the inside. That's it, and keep the legs strong. Use that Buttdar! That's it. Very nice. And when you reach *C*, ask him to come back into trot. Gently does it and . . . *ter-rot.* Very good.'

Noble Warrior slowed down into a rhythmic trot and then to a walk. They turned into the centre of the arena to join Charlie and Percy.

'That's a very good start.' Miss Cameron patted Noble Warrior on the neck. 'Or to be precise, it was a dodgy start, but then you got better. Thatta boy.'

Polly rubbed her leg and then wiped her forehead. She was exhausted.

'It's a very different type of work for a thoroughbred.' The instructor seemed to be talking more to the horse than she was to his rider. 'You

have to learn to use all your muscles, don't you? You've got a good attitude, though, and that helps.' She turned her attention back to Polly. 'And as for you, my girl, you have to use all yours too. Of all the six hundred and fifty odd muscles in your body, you will find that your main strength is in your seat and your back, not your legs. And most of all –' she pointed at her head – 'it's up here, the biggest muscle of all. The brain. That's the bit we need to work on for you and for him. You can't go from winning the Derby to dressage horse all in one go.'

Charlie looked alarmed as Miss Cameron examined her watch.

'Anyway, that will do for today. Well done, both of you. I look forward to seeing you again next week.'

'Does that mean we've passed?' asked Charlie.

Miss Cameron's face was unreadable. She turned to walk back towards the stables and raised a hand above her head.

'Next week! Same time.'

Chapter 10

'Joe's coming to see us!' Larry was waving the iPad in the air as he slid into the kitchen in his socks.

'Whoa, there, son!' Mr Bass tried in vain not to spill his cup of tea as Larry screeched to a halt. Boris barked in surprise and helped to lick up the mess on the floor.

'He's flying over from Ireland to ride at the big meeting next week,' Larry continued, oblivious to the chaos he had caused. 'He'll come down on Monday.'

'That's perfect.' Charlie looked at the calendar on the wall. 'I've got netball practice on Tuesday and Polly's lesson on Wednesday, but Monday is clear.'

She ran down the drive with Boris panting behind her to catch the bus to school.

'Morning, Mrs Wheeler!' she called out cheerily as she swung into the bus.

'Morning, love. Your brothers on their way?' Mrs Wheeler peered past Charlie to see the two boys lumbering slowly up the newly surfaced drive, pushing each other on to the verges as they came. 'In your own time, boys!' she called out.

Harry looked up and sprinted towards the bus.

'Last one there's a *loser*!' he shouted back at his brother, after he'd gained an essential advantage.

Harry reached the bus first. He put his finger and thumb on his forehead in the shape of an L.

Charlie waved at Boris, who barked his goodbye and turned on his heel to trot back down the drive, one hind leg lifted as he hopped along. She wondered if her Border terrier had more brain power than either of her brothers.

'Maybe they'd be more comfortable if I took them in your horsebox!' Mrs Wheeler joked. 'I'm assuming that's why you asked if I could drive it?'

Charlie laughed.

'Don't worry about that, Mrs Wheeler. I've sorted it all out.'

As the school bus pulled into the car park, Charlie saw the dark green Range Rover.

Mrs Williams waved. 'Charlie!' She waved her arm to beckon her over. 'A word, please.'

Charlie's breath caught in her throat. What if Mrs Williams had found out about their secret lesson? She walked over slowly.

'I hear the therapy went very well?' Mrs Williams looked curious rather than cross. 'I'd love to know more about it. Polly was very tired afterwards, but she wouldn't tell me what exercises she'd been doing. We're going to the doctor this afternoon for her latest assessment and I think she'll be impressed.'

Mrs Williams patted Charlie on the back approvingly and then said, 'Polly tells me she's seeing Miss Cameron again on Wednesday. I can cancel my plans and come along. I'm intrigued.'

Charlie's mouth opened and shut, but no words came out.

'You just need to let me know where and when. I'll not cause any bother, I promise. Polly said parents weren't allowed to come to the sessions, but your mother was there, wasn't she?'

'Um . . .' Charlie didn't know what to say. She didn't want to tell an outright lie, but she knew

Mrs Williams would be horrified if she knew Polly was riding Noble Warrior.

'It's c-c-complicated,' she finally stammered. 'You'll have to ask Polly. She might not be ready yet for you to see her . . . performing.'

'Oh? It's a performance thing, is it? I thought it was therapy. I'm not sure Polly is ready to *perform*! She's never liked being judged. Wouldn't that be a bit unfair?'

'Yes, no, well. Um, it is therapy.' Charlie had to think quickly. 'But it's also building up to a performance and I think Polly wants it to be perfect before she can show you.' She smiled in what she hoped was a comforting way. 'Got to dash – going to be late for class.' She didn't allow Mrs Williams the chance to say anything more. She knew she would be in enough trouble without adding more lies into the mix.

She ran into the classroom and slipped into the chair next to Polly just as the bell went for lessons to start. Dr Patterson swept into the room and demanded silence.

'Today we are going to study ourselves.'

Polly and Charlie looked at each other and made a face.

'What?' Polly mouthed.

Charlie shrugged and shook her head.

'Poor body image and low self-esteem are two of the biggest factors affecting the mental health of our pupils,' Dr Patterson went on. 'Who here thinks they have the perfect body?'

One boy put up his hand. He was the captain of the school football team.

'And why do you think that, Eric?' asked Dr Patterson.

'I don't really need to answer that, do I?' Eric replied. He stood up and lifted his arms to flex his muscles. 'You can see for yourself!'

His friends laughed and cheered.

'Thank you, Eric,' said Dr Patterson, 'for demonstrating so clearly the myth of Narcissus.'

'What's that when it's at home?' Eric mumbled.

'*Who* is that, Eric, might be the more pertinent question. He was a beautiful young Greek hunter who fell in love with his own reflection in the water.'

'And what's so wrong with that?' Eric asked as he ran a hand over his cheek and chin. His friends laughed again. 'Totes understandable.'

'He tried to kiss himself and drowned,' Dr Patterson said as she walked towards the windows to pull down the blinds. The rest of the classroom sniggered as Eric abruptly stopped preening himself. Dr Patterson wheeled the large television in front of the white board and turned down the lights.

'I want to use this morning to discuss how we can help each other by building our confidence in the way we look and how we feel about our bodies. First of all, I'm going to show you a film and then we will talk about the issues it raises.'

Polly shifted in her chair. Charlie knew this lesson was not going to be easy for her. She noticed a shape outside the classroom door and wondered who was listening in on the lesson.

Soon she was concentrating on the film, which

showed children of all shapes and sizes while a voiceover explained that all bodies change with age. It also explained how behaviour can change and that hormones create all sorts of strange reactions and emotional swings.

'That must be why Harry and Larry are always fighting,' Charlie whispered. 'It's all that testosterone kicking in.'

Towards the end there was a montage of different people doing sport. They included a girl with an artificial leg, two children zooming along a path in wheelchairs, a swimmer with restricted growth, a single-armed javelin thrower, a one-legged high jumper and a visually impaired sprinter.

'Now,' said Dr Patterson, leaving the room in the dark, 'who thinks they have the perfect body?'

Every single pupil started murmuring in the affirmative.

'Interesting. Let's hear why you've changed your minds,' she said. 'Who wants to go first?'

Polly raised her hand and Dr Patterson nodded at her to speak.

Polly put both her hands on the desk and pushed herself to her feet.

'I used to think my accident had ruined my body and ruined my life.' Her voice was quiet but steady. 'But I am learning to think differently.'

She paused and Charlie squeezed her arm in support.

'I don't want to limit myself by avoiding the things I think I can't or shouldn't do. I don't want to stay out of the room because I'm too scared to join in.'

'Can you give me an example?' Dr Patterson asked.

Polly swallowed and hesitated.

'*Netball*,' Charlie whispered.

Polly laughed nervously, but then said, 'I suppose I need to believe that I can still be part of a team – the netball team, for example – even if it's not as a player.'

'That's interesting.' Dr Patterson looked round the classroom. There was the sound of a chair scraping back and Flora Walsh got to her feet.

'That's a cool idea,' she said. 'We need all the help we can get if we're going to beat St Mary's!'

'I have loads of notes. I can come to every practice session and, if you want me to, I can draw up a training programme –' Polly was talking quickly and confidently now – 'and find out what you should be eating and how much you need to sleep to get the best out of yourselves.'

'Yeah yeah,' came a voice from two rows behind. The words dripped with sarcasm. 'And once you've magically turned us into the best team in the country, I guess you can show us how to do the ladder drill without falling over like your friend.'

Charlie turned round, and even in the darkened classroom she could see Nadia's beady eyes staring at her with hatred. She didn't know what she or Polly had done to deserve such venom.

Polly sat down as fast as she could and bowed her head.

'You have been very brave, Polly. Thank you,' said Dr Patterson.

'That's not brave,' Polly muttered audibly. 'You

should see me riding Charlie's racehorse!'

There was a fraction of a second's pause and then a strangled screech pierced through the door.

'*What?*'

Charlie's blood froze. She thought that silhouette had looked familiar. Mrs Williams had heard every word.

Chapter 11

'You've been riding?' Polly's mother was furious. 'And when exactly were you going to tell me about this? Or indeed ask my permission?'

She glared at Polly. The three of them were standing in the corridor outside the classroom next to the board on which were pinned messages designed to comfort and inspire the pupils.

SOME THINGS TAKE SOME TIME AND EFFORT read one of them.

Too right, thought Charlie.

'It wasn't her idea, Mrs Williams.' Charlie positioned herself so that Mrs Williams could see the message that read I EMBRACE CHALLENGE. 'It's just that she and Noddy have such a good connection and I know, in my heart of hearts, I really know that he would never hurt her.'

'You know that, do you, Charlotte Bass? How? Do you think you're Doctor Dolittle? Can you suddenly talk to the animals? Well, I don't think so – and I don't think you have any *idea* of what a racehorse is capable of doing. Especially one as jumpy as Noble Warrior!'

No one used Charlie's full name unless they were really, really cross. Mrs Williams folded her arms in what Charlie thought was quite an aggressive manner.

'I've seen it first-hand,' she continued. 'I've seen terrible falls on the gallops at home. I've seen how fast racehorses can whip round and gallop off in the opposite direction. They are not playthings!'

Her eyes were sparkling with fury as she turned

on Charlie. 'To think I trusted you. I thought you were trying to help my daughter.'

'She was,' Polly said firmly. 'She *is*. You can't keep me locked away forever, Mum. My head will explode through boredom.'

'Oh, don't be so dramatic, Polly.' Mrs Williams waved her hands in the air. 'I have only ever been concerned about your *safety*. I have always wanted you to achieve great things. What about the netball thing? That's a great idea! You'd be a terrific coach and you like being part of a team. But riding? Well, you know only too well what could happen if you had another fall and I'm just not sure I can bear to watch that happen.'

Polly pushed back her shoulders and looked her mother in the eye.

'And there we have it. *You* can't bear it. Well, I can't bear to live a life without horses – for me that would only be a half-life. I know you are trying to be kind, trying to keep me wrapped in cotton wool, but you are killing me by not letting me ride.'

Charlie backed away. This was clearly a fight

between mother and daughter and she didn't much want to get caught in the crossfire.

'Let's just see what your father thinks about this!'

Mrs Williams turned and marched out to the car park.

Polly leaned against the corridor wall. Charlie saw the sign saying WHY NOT TRY A DIFFERENT STRATEGY? by her right shoulder.

'That went well,' she said.

'Didn't it just?' Polly sighed. 'I didn't know Mum was outside, otherwise I'd never have said a word. She's taking me to the doctor after lunch, so she must have hung around. That'll be a fun afternoon.' She smiled grimly. 'What do we do now?'

The classroom door opened and their fellow pupils started streaming out from Dr Patterson's lesson.

'Nice speech, Polly,' said a boy with frizzy hair.

'You've fooled some of them,' said Nadia as she walked by. 'That's the trouble with the world today – it's full of fake news.'

Charlie rolled her eyes.

Some of the other pupils gave Polly a high five as they walked past her, others said a few words of encouragement or support. Flora Walsh was one of the last to leave the classroom.

'Can you make it to netball practice after school tomorrow?' she asked Polly.

'Sure I can.'

'Make sure you bring your notebook. There's plenty to work on,' Flora said. 'You too, Charlie. I hope we didn't put you off.'

'Oh, don't worry, we'll both be there and Polly's already got plenty of ideas. Just wait until she gets stuck in.'

'See you later, coach,' Flora said as she swung her bag over her shoulder and strode down the corridor.

Later that afternoon at home, Charlie was curled up on her bed reading a book called *Life After Sport* about adapting to a new career after life as an athlete. She was still worrying about how to deal with Polly's mother when the phone rang. The boys were outside, recreating England's World Cup penalty shoot-out against Colombia. Her dad was milking the cows and Charlie didn't know where her mum was, but she certainly wasn't answering the phone. She flung aside her book and ran into her parents' room to pick up. It was Polly.

'What did your mum say?' Charlie asked breathlessly.

'She calmed down after a bit,' Polly explained, 'and eventually I told her that your mum had been keeping an eye on us all the time and we were perfectly safe. I said that all my confidence and balance and whatnot was improving *because* I was riding and that was why I was so happy.'

'Did she get it? Will she let you keep coming here?'

'Yeah. She got it. Kind of. But . . .' Polly paused. 'I haven't told her about the lessons. She doesn't know Miss Cameron is a riding instructor, so make sure your mum doesn't let on. Not until we're ready. I think it would be too much if she knew I was taking it *seriously*.'

'OK,' said Charlie. 'Leave it with me. We'll find a way. See you tomorrow.'

As Charlie hung up the phone, she noticed the book on her mother's bedside table – *The History of the Paralympics*. Charlie knew Polly couldn't give up the one thing that had given her hope and ambition.

From her parents' room, Charlie heard the low roar of an engine. It didn't sound like a tractor or the lorry that came to collect the milk. She looked out of the bedroom window to see a dark blue sports car pulling up. The driver had blond hair poking out of a blue baseball cap. It took her a couple of seconds to register who it was.

Boris had been woken by the noise and he followed Charlie as she galloped down the stairs.

'Love that new surface!' The slender young man swung his legs out, stretching his back as he stood and slammed the door behind him.

'*Joe!*'

Charlie flung her arms round the man who had once been their farmhand, and who had originally taught her to ride. When she had mistakenly bid for Noble Warrior and Percy at an auction, it was Joe who had developed a relationship with the reluctant racehorse. It was Joe who had ridden him to win the Derby at Epsom and Joe who had suggested that Polly should try to ride him.

'So tell me all about working for Seamus O'Reilly. What's it like?' Charlie asked excitedly as she ushered Joe into the kitchen. She made him a cup of tea and they sat across from each other at the big wooden table.

'It's amazing! They told me it was like a five-star hotel for horses, but that didn't help, as I've never stayed in one! I'll tell you what, though, if there's a hotel as nice as Powerscourt Stables, I'll happily stay there for my next holiday.'

'What's so special about it?' Charlie asked.

'Jeez, everything. I swear there isn't a single detail left out.'

Charlie noticed that Joe now had a slight Irish lilt in his voice. He looked more grown up and there was a fire in his eyes, the same energy and excitement she'd seen on Derby Day.

'Each horse has its own set of tack so that germs can't be spread from one to another,' he told her. 'The stables are so lush. Each box is as big as half this room – they've got rubber floors so the horses don't slip; mangers that flip out through the wall so you can fill their feed without walking into the stable; automatic water bowls; fans hanging from the ceiling to keep the air moving in the summer – did you have that brutal summer heatwave here too? – and a heat lamp to keep them warm in the winter. Even the corners of the stables are rounded and the straw is banked up all round.' Joe's eyes were lighting up as he spoke. 'The three-year-old colts have their own yard and they have special stables with a door at the front and the back. The back door leads out into their very own paddock so they can have a pick of grass in the afternoon if they want.'

'Their own paddock?' Charlie was enthralled.

'Exactly. And the grooms only look after three horses each so they get individual attention from the same person every day. Then there's a group of us who ride out on a daily basis – there are ex-champion jockeys and current jockeys and the best work-riders you can find. My dad would have been so impressed. I wish he'd lived to see everything that's happened to me.'

'He'd have loved it.' Charlie put her hand across the table to touch Joe's. 'The main thing is that you're trying to make him proud and that means he's still alive in you. He always will be.'

Joe put his other hand on top of hers and squeezed it.

'How many horses do you ride?' Charlie asked.

'About five or six, so I go almost straight from one to another. Then their groom takes them and walks them for about four miles. Those grooms cover about twelve miles a day, but Mr O'Reilly reckons it's essential that they keep moving with no weight on their backs.'

'I'd be good at that bit.' Charlie patted the top of her thighs. 'These powerful legs were made for walking!'

Joe took a sip of tea, removed his baseball cap

and ran his hand through his hair. Charlie noticed that it was even lighter than usual and his face was bronzed from being outside in the sunshine every morning. 'It's like being at a high-tech university of racing. It's really intense, but I'm loving it.' He grinned broadly and Charlie felt a surge of happiness on his behalf. 'Now you'd better bring me up to date on everything that's happening here on the farm.'

Charlie filled him in on her netball news, including the fact that Polly was going to be their coach, and told him that the boys had finally realized that chickens couldn't dance, but had daft plans for Noble Warrior to open supermarkets. Finally, she told him about Polly trying to ride again.

'We spent ages doing it in secret, but my mum knew all along and now Polly's mum knows, but it's been a bit hairy. I keep worrying that if she has a fall it will all be my fault.'

'That's the risk you both take,' Joe said. 'And Mr O'Reilly always says that there's no reward without a bit of risk. I think it's brilliant news. I always said she and Noddy would work well together. I was worried that she might lose her nerve completely if she didn't get back in the saddle soon.'

'They're learning dressage together,' Charlie explained. 'We found this fantastic teacher who does a lot of work with Riding for the Disabled. She's quite scary and doesn't fuss or give any sympathy. She just makes Polly get on with it.'

Joe nodded and took another sip of tea. 'Can I come and watch?' he asked. 'I'd love to see Noddy strutting his stuff. I can imagine him as a dressage horse – he always had wonderful balance so I would think it suits him. How's Percy, by the way?'

'Oh, still hungry.' Charlie grabbed a couple of apples from the bowl in the middle of the kitchen table. 'I'm trying to keep his snacks healthy. Come on! Let's go out and see them.'

Charlie and Joe wandered out into the farmyard. Bill Bass was in his overalls, tinkering with the tractor. He straightened up. 'All right, Joe? Good to see you again!' He enveloped Joe in a warm hug. 'We miss you, lad.' He wiped his hand across his face and left a streak of black grease. 'So chuffed for you, though. Really thrilled to see what you're doing and how beautifully you ride. Everyone says what a wonderful horseman you are and I know your father would've been so proud.'

Joe bit his lip. Bill was the closest he had to a father since his own had died.

'Thanks,' he said quietly and then rapidly changed the subject. 'That's a fancy-looking tractor you've got there.' He gestured at the gleaming green machine.

'You've always been a good judge, Joe. It's thanks to you and Noddy that I could get a new one. I had a look at all those fancy types like Fendt and Lamborghini but it was the good old John Deere that got me in the end.'

Bill went on to describe all the different types of machinery he could attach to the back and the front of the tractor to pick up silage bales, spread manure or pull a wagon loaded with feed.

'We've had to give the cows a special high-protein nut mix as extra feed. Madonna threw a right strop about it and wouldn't touch them to begin with, but now she's right as rain. Taylor Swift loves 'em and you know what Princess Anne is like –'

'Dad, I know you want to tell Joe all about the cows and show him your fabulous tractor, but he wants to see the horses,' Charlie interrupted. 'We'll be here all day if you take him through everything the Green Machine can do.'

Bill chuckled and doffed his cap. 'Right-o, captain!' He winked at Joe. 'She still runs the show!'

He went back to polishing the tractor, which would soon be covered in a whole new layer of muck.

They climbed through the fence and Charlie whistled at Percy and Noble Warrior. Both of them looked up and pricked their ears before trotting over. Percy didn't bother with the niceties of saying hello – he wanted food. He devoured his apple in two bites and was soon searching for more. Noble Warrior went straight to Joe and sniffed his jacket.

He pushed his nose closer, then stood back and gave a gentle whinny.

'He knows it's you,' Charlie said as Joe broke the apple into smaller pieces and offered it to his favourite horse.

'There's nothing quite like him and there never will be. Not even at Powerscourt is there a single horse as intelligent as Noddy.' Joe's admiration for the animal who had changed his life was clear. His face glowed with affection and pride. 'He looks really well, Charlie. He's grown and thickened out and you can see his muscles are developing in his upper neck and in his quarters.'

Joe ran his hand along Noble Warrior's neck and down his shoulder.

'You're growing into yourself, aren't you, fella? There's a good boy, come on, have a cuddle.'

He took the horse's head in his arms and held it into his chest, stroking Noble Warrior behind the ears.

'He's still an old softie at heart. Ah, I've missed you, Noddy, but look at you now!' He turned to

Charlie. 'It's as if he's found an inner strength. You can have all the data in the world, but you can't measure that. You have to feel it.'

Charlie was pleased that Joe could sense Noble Warrior had changed. She thought so too.

'Oh, he can still get scared of his own reflection, but he's learning and I think he's growing up. I was worried he was getting fat and lazy so the boys built that –' she pointed at the dressage arena in the corner of the field – 'and we got to work. Polly drew up the training schedule for him and he's had to get more flexible and use his muscles in a different way. It's like training an athlete to be a gymnast! The same applies to Polly – it's been brilliant watching her grow in confidence.'

She picked a lump of mud from Percy's mane.

'If you can get away from the racecourse in time, we've got another lesson on Wednesday. You can come and see for yourself.'

'I might just be able to get there if I haven't got a ride in the last. I'll do my best,' Joe replied.

'I won't tell Polly, just in case you don't make it. She's got enough to worry about, what with her mother finding out about the riding!'

Charlie ruffled Percy's forelock and turned back towards the house.

'You'd better come and say hello to my brainless brothers,' she said. 'They've been busy most of the day trying to make the pigs do an agility course. They're very proud of themselves and they'll be furious with me if you don't see it.'

As they walked, Joe started thinking out loud.

'Charlie, did you know there are special classes for ex-racehorses at loads of events? They're related to a charity called "Retraining of Racehorses". Might be an option?'

Charlie dug Joe in the ribs. 'It's lucky you're here, Mr Butler. Good idea.'

They rounded the corner of the pigs' field to see Harry dragging poor Elvis over a row of small jumps.

'Come on, Elvis, *hup!*'

Larry was leading the way in an effort to encourage the pig to copy him.

'It's like this, Elvis!' he cried as he ran and leaped over some pallets that were piled up to a height of about two feet.

Larry wasn't looking where he was going because he was too busy calling over his shoulder to a pig that quite sensibly refused to budge. His foot caught in a gap at the top of the pallet and he came crashing down, face first, into a warm, sticky, brown puddle. He lay there as if winded and then slowly pushed himself up with his arms. He was covered from head to toe in sludge.

Joe and Charlie burst out laughing.

Harry dashed over to help his brother and Elvis took the opportunity to run as fast as he could in the opposite direction, squealing as he went.

Chapter 12

Tuesday's netball practice arrived before Charlie had really thought about it. Her knee was still a bit tender, but it was a lot better. Her mother had insisted she rub arnica cream into it every night and that seemed to have helped.

She and Polly walked to the sports hall together, but Charlie hesitated at the door. 'I don't know that I can do this,' she said.

'Remember what you said to me when you were

trying to talk me into riding again and I thought it was impossible?' Polly asked.

Charlie shook her head. She didn't remember.

'You said that I may have to do it differently, but that didn't mean it couldn't be done. So just do it differently. Come on.'

Polly moved towards the door and pushed it open with her shoulder, leading Charlie into the hall.

The first-team players were already doing their warm-up exercises, leaning from side to side and jumping up and down on the spot. Flora Walsh and Helen Danson were helping each other. Flora was lying on the ground with one leg in the air while Helen stretched it back for her. All of the other players had paired up, but Charlie noticed Nadia was on her own. She was lying on her side with one leg bent over the other, pushing her knee with the opposite hand. It looked painful.

'Now's your chance,' said Polly, giving Charlie a gentle push in the back. 'Act confident, even if you don't feel it, and move towards the problem!'

Charlie took a deep breath. The one girl on the team who had been obstructive and downright hostile was Nadia. The one girl who wouldn't include her or Polly was Nadia. Charlie thought she was like a horse that would try to bite or kick you whenever you came close. A bit like Noble Warrior when she first saw him at the sales when he was battering down the stable door and no one could control him. As she was thinking these things, she found she had walked right up to Nadia.

'Hey there,' Charlie said nonchalantly. 'Wanna hand?'

Nadia rolled on to her back, and without waiting for a reply Charlie grabbed Nadia's left ankle and helped her gently push her leg straight up into the air and then flex it back towards her body. Nadia said nothing for twenty seconds. Then she grunted, 'Other leg.'

Charlie lowered Nadia's left leg gently and raised the right one. She repeated the exercise.

'You now,' Nadia said, rolling herself on to her side and then standing up.

Charlie lay down and raised her leg. She suddenly feared that Nadia might bend her leg so far that she would rupture a muscle. She tensed her whole body.

'Relax,' said Nadia as she gently rotated the ankle and then pushed the leg into an upright position.

'Your left leg is stiffer than your right,' said Nadia as she finished the exercise. 'You might want to work on that.'

Charlie didn't know quite how it had happened, but she felt as if they had passed through a door into another room. During catching practice, she found herself doing drills with Nadia – who *didn't* try to obstruct her – and when they got into a practice match, they were on the same side. Every time Nadia got the ball, she passed it to Charlie. They worked together to defend their zone and when Charlie flicked back a pass that was too long for her, Nadia was right there to catch the rebounding ball.

'Excellent work, girls!' said Mrs Kennedy as the practice match finished. 'Especially Nadia and Charlie in defence. You really work well together and I'm impressed with your reading of each other's games. You seem to know when to turn defence into attack or the other way round. Well done, both of you.'

Charlie smiled at Nadia, who nodded her head in return.

'Well, that was a revelation,' Charlie said to Polly as she sat down on the bench beside her.

'I saw,' replied Polly. 'I've filed it under *Communication*.'

'But we didn't really speak,' said Charlie.

'I know. You don't have to. Some of the best communication is done without words.'

'Hey, you!' Flora Walsh bounced over, her face flushed with exertion. 'What did you think?' She sat down next to Polly and looked at her notebook. 'I'm ready for a full debrief.'

Flora listened as Polly spent the next ten minutes going through the various strengths and weaknesses of the team, pointing out moments when there was confusion on the court or when a player didn't move into the space that had been created.

'I can film the next session, if you like,' Polly suggested. 'That way we can analyse things properly.'

'Sounds great,' said Flora. 'We've never been this professional! I mean, we've always taken it seriously and trained hard and all that, but we've never properly *thought* about it.'

'That's what I'm here for,' said Polly. 'I've also drawn up some nutrition tips for everyone – have a look.'

She handed Flora a folder in which was a sheet of paper for each player, detailing the foods that would help them play for longer without getting tired.

'That is so cool,' said Flora. 'I really appreciate this, Polly. Honestly. I'd never realized how much we needed this kind of help. I'd love to have you officially in the team – that's if you want to be?'

Polly didn't hesitate.

'Of course I do!' she said.

The next day, Charlie and Polly's attention turned back to horses. They hatched a plan to get to the lesson with Miss Cameron early. Then they could already be in the arena, ready and warmed-up, so that Noble Warrior was relaxed and wouldn't spook at himself in the mirror. Charlie wanted it to be perfect, in case Joe came to watch.

'Joe says there are special classes for retired racehorses,' Charlie told Polly. 'They're sponsored by that charity, "Retraining of Racehorses". We could enter you in one of those and see whether Noble Warrior can cope.'

'Do you think we're up to it?' Polly asked.

'Well, there's only one way to find out. Let's give it a go and, if it doesn't work out, at least we know we tried.'

'I've left the saddle over there!' Miss Cameron called out, pointing to her right. 'Polly, make sure you join in with the tacking up. It's important that the riders take part in every aspect of the job. Grooming, mucking out, cleaning tack – riding isn't just about climbing on board and galloping off into the distance.'

Polly winced as she pulled on her riding boots. It was quite a palaver to get everything in order and get herself ready, especially if she needed to be fast.

'The more I rush, the harder it gets,' she complained to Charlie. 'I want to help tack up and I've never been one to avoid hard work – in fact I love grooming and mucking out! But it's just not as straightforward as it used to be.'

Charlie flicked a brush over the thoroughbred's mahogany coat before collecting the borrowed saddle and securing it in place.

'Don't worry about it.' She waited for Noble Warrior to stop blowing his tummy out and then hitched the girth up another two holes. 'It'll come in time. We're a team and the whole point is that I'm here to back you up when you need it. Anyway, I enjoy it too!'

She patted Noble Warrior and moved on to the rather more rotund figure of Percy.

'As for you, Perce!' Charlie had to put all her strength into trying to make the girth strap reach from one side to the other. 'We might need some extensions to get this round you!'

She finally got the metal buckle up to a height that just allowed it to slip into the first hole. Charlie exhaled loudly with the effort.

'Either we have to take more exercise or you need to eat less, Percy,' she reproached him. 'This is not the fine physique of an athlete.'

'Now, now – remember what Doctor Patterson

said!' Polly chuckled. She walked forward to help, using a stick for balance. She was trying it out in place of her crutch.

The two girls grinned at each other as they put the final touches to their mounts. Charlie patted Percy's tummy and his eyes seemed to twinkle at her. They were all ready for their lesson.

Charlie and Polly made their way to the arena where Miss Cameron supported Polly as she climbed up the plastic steps and got herself into the saddle. Noble Warrior spooked at his reflection, but this time he didn't rear or scoot across the arena. After a couple of circuits, he took no notice at all.

'Excellent.' Miss Cameron's voice was crisp and clear. 'Now we will use this lesson to see how much further we can push ourselves. Your first attempt was very good, but dressage is an endless well of opportunity. There is always something new to learn, something more to master.'

Polly squeezed Noble Warrior forward into trot

and tried to keep his head low so that his neck rounded into a slight curve.

'*Use that Buttdar!* Feel the movement and ask him to lengthen down the long side!' Miss Cameron was immediately expecting a higher standard than last week from Noble Warrior and Polly.

Percy plodded along behind with Charlie struggling to turn him from a furry ugly duckling into an elegant swan. It was going to be a long and painful lesson for them.

As both girls concentrated on the instructions they were receiving, they failed to notice the dark green Range Rover raising dust as it came racing into the parking area. Miss Cameron wheeled round on her heels as she heard the screech of tyres and the slamming of doors.

Charlie looked across at the car and the three people who had emerged from it. She saw Mrs Williams, who looked to be in a terrible state. Joe was alongside her, his face pale and drawn – and with them was Polly's father.

Chapter 13

Polly slowed Noble Warrior down to a walk, her face anxious. Charlie followed suit and they waited in the centre of the arena to see how the confrontation would unfold. Mr Williams walked towards the fence, where he stood with his arms crossed. Mrs Williams joined him, her face red with tears. Joe stood two paces behind and mouthed, '*Sorry*,' at Charlie.

'What's going on here?' Mr Williams said.

Miss Cameron walked calmly towards the group. 'We have a lesson in progress,' she said crisply. 'And I do not appreciate interruptions when my pupils are concentrating. Unless there has been an emergency, I do not see any reason to suspend our training. Has there been an emergency?'

'No,' said Joe.

'Yes,' said Mrs Williams.

Miss Cameron locked eyes with Polly's mother. 'And what would that emergency be?'

'Her father and I have only recently discovered that our daughter has been riding.' Mrs Williams pointed at Polly. 'And it is our duty to protect her. She is not allowed to ride like this. One fall, one accident and she could be brain-damaged for life. She could be paralysed. She could *die*.'

Miss Cameron put her head on one side and waited.

'Furthermore, she should *certainly not* be riding *him*!' Mrs Williams's arm shuddered as she pointed again, this time at Noble Warrior. 'He nearly killed her in the paddock at Ascot – he's a liability!'

Miss Cameron raised her hand to indicate silence.

'Alex, you tell her!' Mrs Williams retorted.

Mr Williams still had his arms crossed, but he was not frothing at the mouth, as Charlie had imagined.

There was a moment of stillness as the arena seemed to hold its breath. Then he said, 'Let's give her a chance.'

What? thought Charlie. How was he so calm? Polly said he'd hardly let her out of the front door. She had been sure he would be furious.

'Interesting,' Miss Cameron said calmly. 'I will discuss this with you further at the end of the lesson, but we are on the clock.' She pointed at her watch and turned back to the centre of the arena. 'And I don't want to waste their time or mine.' She smiled at the girls.

'Now go large, please, and let's see what we can achieve. *Trot on!*'

Charlie tried not to look at Polly's parents, but it was too tempting. Every time she trotted past them she strained to hear their snippets of conversation.

This was frustrating. Charlie wanted to know exactly what was going on, but every time she turned her head, Miss Cameron shouted an instruction at her.

'Eyes ahead, Charlie. More leg, please!'

Miss Cameron kept her focus entirely on her pupils. Charlie admired her ability to block out the argument that was still raging just outside the arena.

Then she noticed that her mother had taken Mrs Williams away from the arena. They were heading towards the stables.

'Well done, Polly,' called Miss Cameron. 'Now keep that leg on and bend him round it. That's it. Keep him supple. We're looking for elasticity – and use that *Buttdar*! Excellent.'

Joe and Mr Williams stayed leaning on the fence, watching intently. Mr Williams looked relaxed and Charlie could see Joe smiling with pride.

'Now let's try for a little more impulsion. That's power but not pace. That's it. Well done, Polly. He's really moving for you now. Now let's try to

lengthen his stride even more into extended trot.'

Polly sat deep into the saddle and strengthened the contact with Noble Warrior's mouth through her right rein.

'Keep the leg strong! Don't drop your contact on the rein. That's it. Good effort. Ask him clearly, but don't force him. We will never win a battle with a horse if we rely on force. Let's try it again down the other long side.'

Charlie tried to follow suit with Percy, but his

little legs just went faster and faster, putting in more strides at a quicker rate, but not lengthening. She nearly got bounced out of the saddle.

'We need a little more work there!' Miss Cameron observed. 'He needs to convert that body fat into muscle and it will be a different story. It won't take long, believe me, but let's keep trying. It's good for him to have to make an effort.'

The girls rode hard for half an hour in walk, trot and eventually canter. Charlie was concentrating so intensely that she hadn't noticed her mother and Mrs Williams walking back from the stables to watch from a distance.

After helping Noble Warrior and Polly master the transition from walk to canter, Miss Cameron glanced at her watch.

'And let's allow them to walk long and low, let your reins go nice and loose and ask them to stretch right out for the next few minutes. They've worked hard and the warm-down is always crucial. Well done, girls.'

Miss Cameron kept an eye on them as she walked

to the gate and on to the other side of the fence. She beckoned to Mr and Mrs Williams to stand next to her.

'I promised you that we would continue our discussion. I understand you both have concerns.'

Mrs Williams nodded vigorously and Mr Williams put a protective arm round her shoulder.

'I'm impressed with what you've done with Polly, but it *is* dangerous,' Mrs Williams said. 'And it's particularly dangerous on a racehorse.'

'An *ex*-racehorse,' Miss Cameron corrected. 'And to be honest, I've barely done anything at all. It's Polly who has done the work – and credit to Charlie for helping her find the confidence to try it.'

Charlie saw a minibus arriving in the large tarmac area next to their horsebox and watched a group of children cascading out of it, the sound of laughter and excited shrieks carrying across on the air.

'Once a racehorse, always a racehorse,' Mr Williams said, taking his arm away from his wife's shoulder and gesturing towards Noble Warrior. 'In my experience they never lose their speed of reaction or their tendency to whip round on a sixpence. If they choose to gallop off into the distance, they won't be doing it at a steady, sedate pace, they'll be doing it at thirty miles an hour.'

Mrs Williams shuddered as her husband spoke.

Miss Cameron said nothing, just leaned forward on the fence, one arm resting on the top bar. She watched Noble Warrior and Polly walking round the arena. The sweat glistened on his neck and behind the saddle and his head was low. Polly kept patting him on the neck. Her smile was wide.

'I had my own doubts about him, after everything he's been through,' Cecilia Cameron said finally. 'And I appreciate your experience. I do know who you are and your line of work, and I realize that you have both seen far more racehorses in your time than I have . . . But, with respect, I have seen far more children and adults with a range of physical and learning needs.'

She paused and gestured towards the stables.

'I think you've seen the facilities here and I hope

you'll get a chance to talk to some of the other riders who come here for lessons. They will tell you that their lives have been transformed by this place and these amazing creatures.'

Her hand moved down the front of her jacket, smoothing an imaginary crease.

'Just as every human being is different,' she continued, 'I believe every horse is different, and I think they respond to us and our needs. I agree that racehorses are more sensitive – but I think we have on our hands here a particularly sensitive, perceptive and therefore *receptive* animal.'

'You're so right!' Joe almost sang with enthusiasm. 'Noddy's always been special. He's not like other racehorses and, believe me, I've ridden a few good ones this year. None of them are a patch on him for intelligence or kindness. He is different, I promise you, Mrs W.'

'He didn't look that different when he freaked out in the paddock at Ascot, Joe,' said Mrs Williams. 'He looked like a highly strung, rattled racehorse and he nearly knocked my daughter over.'

'Ah, but he didn't, did he?' Joe responded. 'He knew that she was the one he could trust. They've got a bond, believe me. He's always responded to her and he will always look after her.'

Miss Cameron opened the gate and beckoned to Joe, along with Mr and Mrs Williams, to follow her.

'That'll do, girls. Bring them into the centre here.'

Polly turned Noble Warrior into the middle of the arena and brought him to a halt. Charlie and Percy followed suit. Miss Cameron ran her hand down Noble Warrior's face, along his neck and down his shoulder. She addressed Polly's parents.

'What we have here is a remarkable horse and a remarkable human being. Yes, they could both have an accident, and yes, riding is a potentially dangerous activity, but every time you get in a car, you must be aware of the number of accidents on country roads. Does that stop you from using the car to get where you want to go?'

Miss Cameron waited for an answer. Polly's father shook his head gently in response and reached out for his wife's hand.

'It is impossible in life to protect ourselves from every potential danger,' Miss Cameron continued. 'If we did that, we would never get out of bed and the danger then would be bedsores, boredom and depression. Life is for living. It's about taking chances, pushing on through difficulty, and ultimately about doing the things that make our hearts sing.'

Mr Williams looked at his daughter. Her eyes pleaded with him. He squeezed his wife's hand. He leaned in and whispered something in her ear.

Polly dismounted from Noble Warrior and loosened his girths.

'Your daughter is a wonderful rider and she has a very special connection with this horse,' Miss Cameron said. 'I think they understand each other and they are both young, talented and committed. Together they can achieve great things. But . . . they need something else too.' She paused and looked from one parent to the other.

'What's that?' Mr Williams asked.

'They need support. I have seen plenty of children

come here with a range of mobility and riding experiences, but they have won competitions, improved up through the grades, even gone to the Paralympics – because their parents have been willing to support them every step of the way.'

Charlie could sense the crackle in the air. This was the moment when their plan could either move forward or be stopped in its tracks.

She noted the way in which Miss Cameron had handled the situation. She was persuasive and passionate in her argument, but remained calm throughout. And at the end, at the crucial moment, she had handed the power back to Polly's parents. She was not going to tell them what to do, rather leave them to make the decision for themselves. She now realized that Mr Williams had always suspected that Polly would try to start riding again. That was why he'd given her mother his binoculars – to keep an eye on them. Maybe he'd known from the very first day that she was riding Noble Warrior.

'The National Championships take place next month at Hartpury College in Gloucestershire. I think you should come to watch, to see the different levels of competition and the huge variety of riders.'

Miss Cameron made the suggestion as if it was nothing at all. No big deal, just an option for them to consider. Charlie started to make plans in her head. *Why not take Noddy as well – just for the experience?*

Miss Cameron handed Polly her stick so that she could make her way steadily back to the horsebox. Noble Warrior walked slowly beside her and let her lead him with one hand barely touching the reins.

'We make a great team together,' Polly said, loudly enough for her father to hear. 'I can't tell you how happy it makes me, to be riding again. I feel like I can do anything, I can be anyone.'

'Is that what it's like?' Mr Williams asked his daughter.

Polly nodded enthusiastically. She looked at her mother and Mrs Williams blinked hard as if she had something stuck in her eye. Polly patted Noble Warrior on the neck and allowed Charlie to lead him up the ramp into the horsebox.

'I thought I'd never be able to run or walk properly again and now I feel as if I can fly,' Polly explained. 'It's not the same, but it's blissfully, wonderfully, magically different!'

Noble Warrior whickered gently in agreement.

'OK, OK. I give in,' Polly's mother sighed.

'Really?' Polly asked.

Her father put his arm round his wife's shoulder and drew her close.

'Your mother has always worried about you,' Mr Williams said to Polly. 'She doesn't want you to get hurt and nor do I, but I'd rather you were doing these things with our knowledge than behind our backs. I thought you wouldn't be able to resist riding so I made sure Caroline was watching you every minute, in case something went wrong.'

'Did you?' Mrs Williams looked surprised.

'Yes, love. I didn't want you to feel responsible if she had a fall. I knew you'd never forgive yourself, but I also knew Polly would be miserable if she could never ride again.'

Mrs Williams shook her head in mock outrage.

'Mind you,' said Mr Williams, 'if Joe hadn't let slip that he was coming to watch your lesson, I would never have known about it, and then what?'

He looked at Polly and then at Miss Cameron and back.

'I wouldn't have been able to watch you progress or console you when things went wrong – because they will, believe me. I wouldn't have felt part of it at all and that would have been sad for me and for you.'

Charlie stood nervously by the passenger door of the horsebox. Noble Warrior and Percy were safely in the back sharing a hay net that one of them was pulling with force, making the back end of the lorry sway from side to side. Charlie could guess which one.

'As for you, Charlotte Bass, it may take a while for me to forgive you.' Mr Williams sounded stern, but Charlie noticed that his eyes were twinkling.

'I'm sorry we didn't tell you sooner, Mr Williams.

In my defence, I didn't think dressage was your thing.'

Alex Williams snorted. 'Trust you to have a quick excuse. You're right, I don't know a *passage* from a *piaffe*, but I do know what makes my daughter happy and I'll give you credit for that. I haven't seen her smile so much since before her accident and that's good enough for me to buy into this daft idea!'

Polly climbed into the Range Rover to go home with her parents while Joe hopped into the front seat of the horsebox to travel back to Folly Farm.

'Mum, I'm sorry we put you in such an awkward position. I know we should have told Polly's parents,' Charlie said as they drove steadily out of the riding centre.

'I wouldn't worry too much,' her mum said. 'Alex knows his own daughter and he was on to her before she'd even tried to ride properly. I think he's fine. As for Jasmine, she'll come round to it all. I showed her the stables and introduced her to a few of the volunteers and the women who were in the lesson when we arrived.' She flicked the indicator on. 'They were brilliant at explaining what a difference it had made to their lives and how their bodies were more supple. They also told her how much it had done for their confidence and I suspect that's what really tipped the balance. She's been worried about Polly's self-esteem and her loss of ambition. To be honest, I think she's been far worse at home than she is when she stays with us. Maybe that's why her dad realized that taking away her riding was destroying her.'

Charlie saw a magpie flying into the hedgerow ahead. She saluted with her right hand.

'I still thought she might say no,' her mum continued. 'But when she saw how different Noble Warrior looked and how much Polly was enjoying trying to turn him into a dressage horse . . . I think she figured it was doing both of them good.'

'Thanks for taking her round the stables, Mum,' Charlie said. 'That gave us time to get Noddy going in the arena. Once he warms up he can hold a really good outline. Wait till he gets to perform to music and I think he will really start dancing!'

Chapter 14

They spent the rest of the journey discussing the various elements of freestyle dressage and how important it was to find a beat and a rhythm that suited the horse. Some music was just too slow and some too irregular.

'It needs to be strong and upbeat,' Charlie said.

'I think it needs to mean something too,' Joe added. 'You'll know when you find it because it'll make the hairs on the back of your neck stand up.'

They reached the farm after dark and Mrs Bass beeped the horn to let the boys know they were back. They came running out of the farmhouse to help them unload.

'We've had fun and games today!' Charlie told them. 'Looks like we've got a big championship to get ready for.'

'I thought we were just going to watch?' her mother interjected.

Charlie looked at her and tried to raise her eyebrow.

Mrs Bass laughed. 'You'll get it one day, my love!'

Harry pulled the ramp down and started to open the first partition.

'That'll keep us on our toes!' he said. 'On our toes! Get it? Like a ballet dancer. . . ha ha!' He made himself laugh so hard that he couldn't stop Percy barging past him and charging down the ramp.

Joe had time for a very brief supper before he had to head back to the airport. He willingly accepted a slice of brie and marmalade flan.

218

'This is such an original mix. Very ... *interesting*,' he said as he tentatively moved the flan round his mouth. 'I've really missed this. The food at Powerscourt is pretty tame by comparison. It's nice, but it's never ... surprising.' He took another mouthful and gave an impressed nod. 'Really, it's better than it looks!'

As Joe got ready to leave, Charlie was still thinking about the dressage routine for the National Championships when he asked, 'Have you seen the film *The Greatest Showman*?'

'*Yes!* It's brilliant. Polly and I have seen it four times so far. I think it's the best film I have *ever* seen.'

'What about the music?' Joe asked as he opened the car door. 'Don't you think it would be perfect for Noddy?'

Charlie felt that surge of electricity that happened when she was really excited about a brilliant idea.

'OMG, you're a genius, Joe Butler! Of course that's the answer. I can just see him trotting down the centre line to "This Is Me"! I can't wait to see what Polly thinks!'

She kissed him on the cheek and shut the front door as he revved up the engine and spun the car round to head down the drive. Charlie waved him goodbye and ran back into the farmhouse, full of creative energy.

As soon as she got the green light from Polly, planning became Charlie's major assignment. She loved making lists, and with her mother's help she devised a timetable for Polly and Noble Warrior that would prepare them for a dressage test to music at the National Championships. What Polly was doing for her and the netball team, Charlie would repay by doing the same.

Charlie rang the organizers and tried to enter Polly and Noble Warrior. It was long past the deadline so she had to make their entry *hors concours*, which meant they weren't allowed to win any prizes, but they could still be judged and their score compared to everyone else's.

Charlie had read in her *Horse & Hound* that the Paralympic selectors always went to the National Championships to see if there was any new talent. She was certain that Noble Warrior and Polly would put on a performance that they couldn't ignore.

Harry and Larry got to work on the computer to create a medley of songs from *The Greatest Showman* that they could play from the portable speakers so that Polly could get used to the changes in rhythm and plan her moves accordingly. Finally they had found an outlet for their shared interest in choreography. They had no idea how relieved the chickens would be to be released from their dance lessons.

The test needed to show the best of Polly and Noble Warrior so they made sure it included two sections of extended trot across the diagonal line of the arena, plus a walk-to-canter transition that could really flaunt his fluency. Charlie was genuinely impressed with the effort her brothers were putting in. She couldn't believe they cared so much.

They were watching with her as Polly went through the test in the arena they had built.

'Um, Charlie?' Harry said tentatively.

They were standing to the side of the arena, watching Polly practise the walk-to-canter transition.

'Try that again, Pol!' Charlie shouted. 'He's just starting to anticipate it a bit. Do it on the other corner so he doesn't know it's coming.'

She kept her eyes on Polly, but cocked her

head towards her brother. 'Yeah?'

'Well, it's about One Market . . .' Harry said.

'One Market?'

'The supermarket – the one that's opening in Andover. They've been back in touch with another offer since we kind of let the conversation slide.'

Larry was taking photos of Noble Warrior on his phone to upload to the blog later on. He looked on his screen and zoomed in on the picture, lightened it and added a sparkle effect.

'That looks much better!' Charlie shouted at Polly. She glanced back at Harry.

'They've kept our fee the same, but they've also offered to make a significant donation to Wilmington RDA,' he said with a grin.

Charlie stopped looking at Noble Warrior and turned to face him fully. 'What?'

'Well, they want Polly to come as well, you see. They are changing the way their supermarkets look and feel. They want to make it fully accessible and they don't just mean parking and electric doors. They've got buttons to press to lower things from shelves that are too high to reach.'

'Wow!' said Charlie. 'I'd never even thought about that.'

'*And* they're putting audio guides on every aisle,' Harry added. 'So you can get an app on your phone or they give you this special scanner that reacts to voice command so when you point it at something, it can explain what it is and how much it costs. They've also got Braille labels on everything.'

Polly finished her practice test by trotting down the centre line and halting. As she saluted to an imaginary judge, Larry snapped another photo while Harry and Charlie started clapping.

'That's beginning to look really polished,' Charlie said as Polly walked towards them, patting Noble Warrior on the neck.

'He can do it, he *really* can,' said Polly. 'And he loves that music. He reacts to it as if it was written just for him.'

'*Keeeep dancing!*' the boys said together.

Charlie smiled. Trust them to bring it all back to *Strictly*.

'*The Racehorse Who Learned to Dance* is the new title of Harry's blog,' Larry explained. 'The latest post had more hits than anything we've written before. People love it and I think that's why One Market came back with a better offer. I've told Polly about it and she's keen, aren't you?'

Polly nodded.

Charlie was thinking. Maybe she'd been a bit of a snob about the supermarket idea. She hadn't liked the thought of Noddy being exploited, but this . . . sounded like a really positive idea. And if they were going to give a large donation to Wilmington RDA, there was even more reason to say yes. They had a waiting list as long as her arm of children and adults who wanted lessons. With a good chunk of money, she knew Miss Cameron could buy another pony, build more stables or take on another member of staff so that they could help more people.

'When do they want to do the grand opening?' Charlie asked.

Harry looked at Larry, who looked at Polly, who looked back at Charlie. They waited. Eventually Harry asked, 'Does that mean you're saying yes?'

'Well, I'm not saying no . . .'

Larry clapped his hands together. 'It's next month, just a couple of days after the National Championships.'

Charlie grimaced. It was a lot to expect of Noble Warrior: two public appearances within days of each other when he'd hardly been out of the field for a year.

'I think it could work really well,' Polly said. 'We do the Nationals and then he gets a day off to relax and then it's only a couple of hours in Andover to stand there and get patted by everyone. He'll enjoy the attention.'

'They know Percy has to come too?' Charlie asked her brothers.

'Yup,' said Larry. 'I told them he's the food expert in the family!'

Chapter 15

Charlie was selected as wing defence for the first netball match of the season against their local rivals, St Mary's. They were the best team in the area and hadn't lost a match for two years.

Nadia played goal defence. Polly gave the team a warm-up routine that made them concentrate on changing direction and anticipating the next pass. At the end of their warm-up, the team huddled together in a giant circle, their arms round each other. Charlie found she was next to Nadia, and Polly and Mrs Kennedy were also in the cluster.

'I know it's only the first match of term,' said Mrs Kennedy, 'but I've seen an improvement in training that is really exciting – so go out there and enjoy yourselves. Nadia, you and Charlie are bringing out the best in each other so keep that up.'

Charlie felt Nadia pat her on the back.

'And there was me thinking you were going to steal my place,' Nadia said softly. 'And instead we are making each other better than we would be on our own.'

Ah, thought Charlie. There it was.

'Polly, would you like to say a few words?' Mrs Kennedy asked.

Polly coughed and looked around the huddle, searching their faces.

'I need you to start reading each other's minds and we can only do that by getting to know every team mate really well,' she said. 'Don't be afraid to try things, and if they don't work, that's fine. I'd rather we aimed to be inventive and made the odd mistake than stayed safe and got beaten anyway.'

Polly put one hand into the centre of the circle, holding on to her crutch with the other. Everyone else put their hand on top of hers. They pushed down and up, shouting together, *'One team, one dream!'*

Polly made her way back to the bench and picked up her notebook. The whistle blew and the game started. Trainers squeaked and team mates shouted as the ball flew around from hand to hand. It was a tight match and, going into the final quarter, there were two points in it.

'We can do this!' Flora Walsh implored her team mates. 'We're only just behind.'

'Remember the Roses!' said Polly. 'Play right to the whistle. Don't stop for anything or anyone until that final whistle has finished blowing. Keep taking risks and keep moving into the spaces. Feet, focus, fitness!'

'That's good,' said Nadia to Charlie. 'Where does she get this stuff?'

'I have no idea,' replied Charlie. 'But I swear she sees things that no one else sees. She can make the difference, as long as you listen to what she's saying.'

'Oh, don't worry, I'm listening,' said Nadia as she ran back towards her court position.

With twenty seconds on the clock, St Mary's were one point ahead and on the attack. Nadia blocked the final pass and parried the ball to her left. Charlie was there to collect the rebound and quickly passed on to Flora Walsh at centre. Flora took a step forward and, without looking, passed the ball into the space to the left of the shooting circle. Helen Danson, goal attack, stretched an arm out and with her fingertips clawed the ball into her grasp. St Mary's massive goalkeeper tried to block her path, but Helen faked a shot and, in the same move, passed sideways to the goal shooter, a tall girl called Daisy Bushell. Daisy took a step closer to the net and calmly slotted the ball away.

The scores were level. Flora shouted for the ball, which was swiftly returned to her to start again. The clock was ticking down as she flicked the ball forward out of the centre circle. Charlie moved up to help in the central zone and looped a high pass towards the net. Helen Danson plucked it out of the air and, with two seconds left on the clock, took a shot. The ball bobbled round the top of the ring, trying to make up its mind whether to drop. The umpire put the whistle to her lips and started to blow as the ball fell through and into the net. *Goal!*

Polly grabbed her stick as she leaped up in celebration. The subs and Mrs Kennedy rose as one and the team rushed over to join in the melee.

Nadia's arms reached round Polly and lifted her on to her shoulders.

'Hold tight!' she shouted.

Charlie felt the rush of pride, adrenalin and elation that she had last experienced when Noble Warrior won the Derby. This time it was herself and Polly she was thrilled for, rather than Joe and Noddy. She grinned up at her friend, high on Nadia's shoulders, and joined in the dancing with Flora, Helen, Daisy and Mrs Kennedy.

An hour later, Polly and Charlie were still buzzing. And a week later, they were still talking about it – and the whole school knew that Polly Williams was the secret of their success.

Chapter 16

On the evening before the National Championships, Charlie and Polly cleaned all the tack for Noble Warrior and Percy. They prepared a hay net, washed out the horsebox and folded all their riding clothes neatly into a bag so that there was no danger of their cream jodhpurs getting dirty on the way to Hartpury College. They woke up an hour before they needed to and crept downstairs with all their kit.

'We can give the horses an early feed and I'll plait Noddy's mane while he's eating,' suggested Charlie. 'You can do his tail in a French plait. That'll look smart.'

By the time Mrs Bass came out with two cups of tea, Noble Warrior looked like he'd been to an equine beauty salon.

'All set?' she asked.

'All set,' replied the girls in unison.

'Dad's going to bring the boys later and, Polly, your parents will meet us there. We ought to arrive early, I think – give Noddy time to get his bearings and settle in.'

Boris barked.

'Of course you can come, Boris. It wouldn't be a proper outing if you weren't with us!'

Boris chased his tail, spinning round in a circle in celebration. He rushed ahead to the horsebox and was sitting proudly in the passenger seat by the time Charlie led Percy up the ramp. Polly waited with Noble Warrior. They had worked out a good routine and Charlie scampered back to grab him before Percy got too restless on his own.

They set off to Gloucestershire full of nervous excitement. They didn't stop talking the whole way and it was only when they drove into the car park at Hartpury College that Charlie appreciated how big an event it was. There were hundreds of horseboxes and trailers and, all around them, adults and children were riding horses and ponies. By the side of nearly all the vehicles, Charlie noticed wheelchairs, crutches and walking sticks.

Polly's eyes widened.

'There are so many competitors,' she gasped. 'I don't think I can do this.'

Some ponies were being led by people in sweatshirts with the names of different RDA groups. Charlie watched a girl of about ten riding with an adult on each side.

'Come on. *You can*,' said Charlie softly. 'Remember how you got the best out of the netball team? We didn't think we could beat St Mary's and you convinced us that we could. I'm here, and Mum's here, and we're your team.'

Mrs Bass parked the horsebox and the girls tumbled out, followed closely by Boris.

A woman's voice came over the tannoy. 'Arena Four for the Class Two dressage, starting at nine thirty. Arena Four, please.'

'I think our class is the one after that.' Mrs Bass had checked the website for information. 'There are quite a lot of riders in Class Two so I would think we've got a little while, but we need to go to the secretary to confirm our entry. I can do that while you girls get ready. How does that sound?'

'Thanks, Mum, that would be great.' Charlie swallowed, but her mouth was dry. She felt like she had on the morning of the Derby, and even if today's dressage test wasn't worth a million pounds, she knew it was just as important, if not more so. She was nervous for her friend, but she couldn't afford to show it.

Boris jumped up at her legs.

'What is it? What have you seen?'

Boris barked and looked towards the horsebox next door. There was a golden retriever sitting calmly by the side of the ramp. The dog had a harness and a bib saying, GUIDE DOGS. A girl in dark glasses patted the dog on the head. She was wearing jodhpurs and a tweed hacking jacket. She adjusted her riding hat and did up the chinstrap.

'She must be blind.' Charlie pointed her out to Polly.

'What adjustments do you think she uses for riding?' Polly asked.

'I reckon we're about to find out.'

The girl took the harness of her dog and walked behind it to the other side of the horsebox. A moment later she appeared again, this time on the back of a beautiful bay horse.

'Will you bring Rufus, Mum?' she called behind her.

'Will do,' came the reply as her mother locked the horsebox, removed the harness from the golden retriever and set off behind her daughter, who rode down a wide path between the trailers, cars and horseboxes towards a large field.

'As you said, I guess you just get on with it.'

Charlie pointed at a boy who was manoeuvring himself out of a power chair and up into the saddle. He gathered up his reins and rode off. 'See, he knows he's a rider who simply needs a bit of help getting on board. Everyone here is a rider, first and foremost.'

'That's what it is!' Polly exclaimed suddenly. 'They're here because they *can* ride, not because they can't run.'

She held up her hand. Charlie high fived her. They changed into their cream jodhpurs and pulled on clean, shiny brown boots. Charlie helped Polly do up her Pony Club tie. She took a step back to admire her friend.

'You look hot to trot!' she laughed.

Charlie held out her arm as Polly climbed on to the portable mounting block they'd brought with them, and held Noble Warrior as Polly manoeuvred herself into the saddle. Charlie checked the girths, double-checked that the stirrup leathers were the right length and patted the gleaming black neck of her Derby winner.

'Now you remember, Noddy, you're not a racehorse any more. There's no need to panic or get uptight. It's dressage, not *stress*-age.'

She turned back to the side of the box where Percy was tied up. Or rather, where he *had been* tied up. There was no sign of the porky Palomino.

'Oh no!' she exclaimed. 'Don't tell me someone's been daft enough to kidnap Percy. They'll soon regret it. Where has he gone?'

Boris ran to the front of the horsebox. He barked and ran back to Charlie before disappearing round the front again. Charlie took the hint and followed him to find Percy with his head through the window of the passenger side, helping himself to the picnic her mother had brought.

'You greedy monster! That's not your lunch. Come on, get out of there.'

Charlie pulled at the reins, forcing Percy to bring his head back through the window. He was munching on a cucumber sandwich and was clearly miffed he wouldn't have a chance to finish the picnic all in one go.

'I see you've left the bananas. Had enough of them for one lifetime, have you?'

Charlie couldn't be cross with him for long, especially as he was chewing so delicately on his cucumber sandwich. She had to admire his ingenuity. He'd got his head through a narrow gap in the window and forced it wide enough open for him to stretch through and pull the bag closer before carefully opening the zip and removing the items one by one.

'I reckon you were a jewellery thief in another life. If you had fingers rather than hooves, I can only imagine how dangerous you'd be. Now come on, we've got a dressage test to supervise.'

Polly and Charlie rode towards the warm-up area, where they found even more riders practising their routines. They saw the girl from the car park responding to her mother's directions, working in perfect synchronicity with her horse. They saw the boy encouraging his pony to trot sideways in a half-pass.

'Let's go over to this end to warm up,' Charlie

said, pointing to the far corner of the field. 'There's more space.'

Charlie watched as Polly walked and trotted Noble Warrior in circles round her. She shouted occasional suggestions, but Polly pretty much had it under control.

She could see Noddy's neck becoming rounder and his back end getting more active as his muscles warmed up. Polly moved into canter and encouraged him to stretch and then shorten, changing the length of his stride. They looked magnificent. Polly brought Noddy back through his transitions from canter to trot, and trot to walk, before halting and patting him on the neck.

'He's lovely and relaxed,' said Charlie as Polly walked back towards her. 'You look fantastic together and, whatever happens in the arena, you've come such a long way.'

'He's the one doing all the work,' replied Polly. 'I'm just sitting here, telling him what to do. He's adapted so well and I think he's enjoying it.

He feels so much more confident and he doesn't even look for Percy the way he once did.'

Charlie spotted her mother, Boris wagging his tail alongside her. Her dad had arrived with Harry and Larry, sporting matching RDA baseball caps. She had no idea where they had got them. Charlie also saw Polly's parents on the bank above the warm-up area. They were standing close together and she thought she could see them holding hands.

'Hey, girls! Are you nearly ready?' Charlie's mum called out. 'They're about to call Class Three, which is you. I've checked us in and found the arena so I think we're all set.'

'Thanks, Mrs Bass,' said Polly. 'You've been an absolute rock. We wouldn't have got here without you.'

'Oh, I don't know,' Mrs Bass replied. 'I reckon you two would have got yourselves exactly where you wanted to be, with or without my help –'

The tannoy cut across them.

'*Class Three* starting now in Arena *Four*. All competitors for Class Three to Arena Four *immediately.*'

Chapter 17

As they made their way towards Arena Four, with Percy leading the way, Charlie heard a commotion. She glanced over to see about twenty carriages rumbling towards one of the other arenas. She looked back at Noble Warrior nervously. This was just the sort of thing that would terrify him.

He pricked his ears and looked in the direction of the carriages.

Polly spoke to him calmly. 'It's all right, boy. No one can hurt you here. They're off to a competition, just like us. Good boy, that's the way.'

From nowhere appeared a slim, upright figure in blue. Miss Cameron was suddenly walking on the left side of Noble Warrior. She didn't grab at his head or even tug on the rein. She just let her hand rest on it, giving Polly and Noble Warrior reassurance. Charlie gulped.

'*Miss Cameron?* I had no idea you'd be here.'

'The organizers rang me to check some details,' she said. 'You'd put Wilmington RDA as your club so they cross-referenced with me.'

Charlie was dismayed. She hadn't told Miss Cameron that she had entered Polly and Noble Warrior. She didn't want her to think that she had gone behind her back.

'Clever idea, by the way.' Miss Cameron looked at Charlie and winked. 'To enter *hors concours*. That way you can find out what standard you've reached, without the pressure of trying to win.'

Polly started humming the tune to 'Never

Enough', the most serene song she could think of from *The Greatest Showman.*

Noble Warrior dropped his head and seemed to relax as they made their way towards Arena 4. They watched the first couple of competitors ride their tests, which were impressively smooth and accurate. Charlie was nervous on Polly's behalf. She could feel her heart rate increasing and thought she'd better move away in case Polly could hear it pounding.

'I'll be right behind the judge's car at *C*,' she told her friend. 'That's as close as I'm allowed to be, but at least Noddy will know we're there. Are you feeling OK?'

Polly nodded. Her face had gone pale and her lips were pursed in concentration.

'Don't try to hide Noddy's failings, just show off his strengths,' said Miss Cameron. 'You can do this.'

Polly winked and said, 'What failings?'

'Attagirl.' Miss Cameron smiled.

Polly sat tall in the saddle and put her shoulders back. She took a deep breath and, when the judge beeped her car horn, she nodded at Harry to start the music. The opening chords of 'This Is Me' rang out as she entered at A and trotted up the centre line. She halted at X and Charlie smiled at her as she elegantly dropped her right hand and bowed her head in salute.

Noble Warrior was loose and lithe, moving like a ballet dancer across the turf as he sprang from walk into trot, circled and crossed the diagonal, moved forward into a bouncy but relaxed canter. The drumbeats matched his hooves striking the ground and the lyrics summed up everything that Polly had overcome and everything she believed in.

'I make no apologies, this is me!'

Noble Warrior's ears flicked backwards and forwards as he listened to Polly's voice and to the music. His head remained low, his mouth working the bit as he responded to her hands. The music switched to 'A Million Dreams' for the slower paces and then to 'Come Alive' before switching back for the last section to 'This Is Me'.

As Polly came up the centre line for the last time and into her final halt, Charlie realized she had

been holding her breath. The crescendo to the last words of the song timed perfectly with Polly's salute to the judges. Charlie exhaled and sang out loud, '*This is me!*' as Polly patted Noble Warrior and smiled to every corner of the arena.

Charlie was sure that the applause from the spectators was louder than for any of the previous competitors and she could hear whooping and whistling. She glanced at the crowd and then quickly back to Noble Warrior to check the noise hadn't alarmed him. He was on his toes, but there was no danger of him boiling over. Polly was in full control as they walked out of the arena.

As she trotted over to shower Polly with praise, Charlie noticed a small group of people in blue blazers with red-white-and-blue silk scarves. They were writing into hardback notebooks. She switched her attention back to her friend.

'*Wow, wow, wow!* That was perfect!' Charlie couldn't contain her excitement. 'That was so much better than anything we've done at home or at Wilmington, and if you don't get a ten for that final halt, there is no justice in this world. Oh my word, it was *breathtaking*!'

Polly raised her head and looked up to the skies, her eyes full of tears. She then fell forward and buried her face in Noble Warrior's mane. Charlie couldn't hear much of what she said, but made out the words 'thank you', 'legend' and 'epic'. Eventually Polly turned her head sideways and Charlie could hear what she was saying. 'Did you see the mistake I made in the canter? I started it early and then stopped and started again. It was totally my fault, but they're bound to deduct points for that.'

'Never mind.' Charlie patted her on the knee. 'That's just one tiny mistake. I didn't even notice! The rest was just brilliant and you looked so confident.'

Miss Cameron was beaming from ear to ear with a show of emotion Charlie had not seen from her before.

'For a first effort in public, that really was the greatest show.' She patted Noble Warrior on the neck and smiled at Polly. 'Congratulations, my dear.

You have revealed to the world that this is most certainly *you!*'

Soon Polly and Noble Warrior were surrounded by well-wishers. Polly's mother looked up towards her daughter sitting tall in the saddle.

'It was beautiful. You were magnificent and so was Noble Warrior.' Mrs Williams sniffed as she spoke.

'As you know, I don't really understand dressage,' said Mr Williams. 'But from what I could see it looked very good, if a little slow for my liking.'

'It's *meant* to be slow, Dad! It's the exact opposite of racing!'

Miss Cameron slipped away from the throng and Charlie noticed her talking with a grave face to one of the blazer-wearing women she had seen taking notes. Charlie was confused. Had they done something wrong?

An hour later, once they'd finished what was left of the picnic, they wandered down to the enormous tent in the middle of all the arenas. Around them were dressage classes still in progress, a show-jumping arena and a gymkhana with ponies bending in and out of vertical poles, and kids picking apples out of buckets of water with their teeth.

'There's a lot going on, isn't there?' said Mrs Williams. 'I had no idea there even was a Riding for the Disabled National Championships.'

'They have all sorts of classes,' Charlie explained, 'from those who are just beginning to the really high achievers. They're the ones who go to the Paralympics.'

They went into the main marquee where about sixty riders were waiting for their scores to be written on to the white boards that lined the sides. Some of them were in wheelchairs, others on crutches, and all of them were talking about horses.

'Any score above sixty-five per cent would be amazing,' Charlie said to Mrs Williams. 'I thought it looked perfect, but I didn't see all the other tests so I don't know how we compare. It's all down to the judges and whether they liked what they saw.'

'Much more complicated than a race, isn't it?' said Mr Williams. 'I like knowing I've won as soon as my horse crosses the line. I don't much fancy waiting for the judge to decide if he liked the way my jockey looked as he was riding a finish!'

'Shh, Dad!' Polly batted an arm at him. 'Just because you don't understand it doesn't mean you have to mock it.'

'I'm not mocking it, love. I'm just glad my sport is more straightforward. I'm a simple fellow, Polly!' He gave her a big grin and Polly smiled back.

Miss Cameron reappeared just as the numbers started to be written on the board. Her posture was perfect – shoulders back, spine straight, legs firm. *If it wasn't for her knobbly finger*, thought Charlie, *Miss Cameron could be drawn with straight lines*. Even her hair didn't have any kinks or curves.

Charlie held Polly's arm as the numbers went up. 60%, 62.4%, 59%, 68.7% and then, next to Noble Warrior's name – 68.33%.

'Hurray!' they all cheered together and the woman writing up the scores turned round to give them a stern look. Then she carried on writing, following Noble Warrior's score with *HC*. Charlie heard another competitor say 'Phew!'

'That's an amazing score for your first ever test!' Charlie tried to sound calm, but she was too excited.

'There's bound to be a few better than that,' Polly replied. 'After all, I made a mistake!'

They watched the marks go up for the rest of the class. There were a couple on 69% and then, right at the end, the very last score went up – 73%. It was a rider Charlie knew was on the Paralympic squad.

'You'd have finished fifth!' Charlie said. 'That's incredible. No disgrace in that. The winner got medals in London and Rio. Mind you, if you make a mistake in your test again, I'll have to sack you!' she joked.

'That's what we like to hear. Competitive spirit.' A woman in a blue blazer had approached them. She was wearing a red-white-and-blue silk scarf and she had a metal pin on the lapel of her blazer. It said PARALYMPICS GB. She thrust out her hand and spoke in a strong, confident voice.

'Marjorie Pearson. You can call me "Mrs P". Everyone does. Pleased to meet you, Polly.'

Polly shook her hand, trying to mask a look of confusion.

'Cecilia Cameron has told me she thinks you are a real talent. You have potential, she says, and when Miss Cameron tells us that about a rider, I have to tell you – we listen.'

'She has been really helpful,' Charlie said.

'And you are?' Mrs P looked at Charlie.

'This is Charlie Bass.' Polly said. 'She's my fr– um, she's my team captain. As I'm sure you know, we all need a team around us to make this happen.'

Polly gestured at everyone in the tent who was there to support their riders – parents, friends, RDA volunteers, guide dogs. None of the competitors were alone.

'Excellent,' said Marjorie Pearson. 'All the best riders have a captain of the ship. This one's a bit younger than most, but she's clearly done a good job. Now I need to have a little chat with you and your parents, if that's possible.'

'They're just here.' Polly called her mum and dad over.

'Good. Excellent. Well, gather round, team, I have news and I have questions.' Marjorie Pearson was clearly used to addressing large numbers. 'Questions first. I need to know whether any of you eat sushi?'

Charlie looked at Polly, who looked at her parents, who looked at Mr and Mrs Bass, who looked at Harry and Larry, who looked at Miss Cameron. What was this woman going on about?

'No? Ah well, never mind. I'm from the Podium Potential Programme. Mrs P from the PPP. Ha ha! Add another P for Paralympics and it trips off the tongue rather, doesn't it?'

Charlie noticed that Mrs P said 'orf' rather than 'off' and that she pronounced *potential* in a very strange manner.

'Anyway, my job is to spot *po-ten-shee-al* for the Paralympics and you, my dear, you *def-i-nite-lee* have *po-ten-shee-al*. What say you let us sign you up for our programme?'

Polly didn't know what to say.

'Can I ask what it entails?' Charlie stepped in as her friend had momentarily lost the ability to speak.

'Well, for one thing, we will pay all the costs of her lessons with a specially selected coach, and cover any veterinary bills, any equipment costs, any travel expenses. In fact, we will do everything in our power to make sure that Polly and that gorgeous horse can be in a position to compete in a future Paralympic Games, if she shows the right commitment and improvement and is selected for the British team.'

Polly's mother started to wobble and had to be supported by Alex Williams. Harry and Larry were nudging each other in amazement. Even Miss Cameron looked a little surprised.

'We would like to take you to Tokyo on a fact-finding mission,' continued Mrs P. 'We do it with the youngsters we think will benefit from seeing how it all works. I know you are a fan of *The Greatest Showman* so you will appreciate that it is a bit like a large travelling circus. We have to make sure every member of the team feels confident and prepared to the very highest level so that they can perform in the big ring.'

Charlie was trying to compute all of the information Mrs Pearson was sharing. She'd had an instinct that riders could be spotted at a very young age – Sophie Christiansen had won a gold medal at only sixteen – but it still felt unreal.

Mrs Pearson was waiting for an answer.

'What say you?' She honked the question like a goose.

'What say they? Well, they'd be darned idiots to say anything other than *hai onegaishimasu* and *arigatou*.' Miss Cameron finally spoke.

'What?' said Charlie and Polly together.

'It's Japanese for *yes please* and *thank you*.'

'You speak Japanese?' Charlie asked.

'I spent a summer at the Kaminokawa Horse Park, helping them to establish their own Riding for the Disabled programme. They are exceptional in their attention to detail and I think the

Paralympics in Tokyo could be the best-organized games ever.'

Charlie shook her head. She never ceased to be impressed by the experiences people had that took them out of their ordinary lives. There was clearly even more to Miss Cameron than met the eye.

'Can Miss Cameron be our coach?' Charlie asked.

Mrs P hesitated. 'Miss Cameron is certainly very highly regarded by the PPP. She has all the necessary coaching qualifications, and although she is not currently on our list of Paralympics GB coaches . . . I do not see why not.' Mrs P addressed Miss Cameron directly. 'Would you be prepared to take Polly on as a project?'

Charlie and Polly both looked at Miss Cameron. She bowed her head.

'Is that a yes, Miss Cameron?' Polly asked.

Cecilia Cameron ran her hand along the side of her slicked-back hair.

'I would be honoured to be your coach,' she said.

Polly threw her arms round Miss Cameron. Both

her parents and Charlie's parents joined in the group hug and Harry gave Larry a high five before picking up Boris to kiss him on the nose.

200,000

Chapter 18

The next day, Larry uploaded the photos from the National Championships and wrote an update to *The Racehorse Who Learned to Dance*. He added a video of part of Polly's freestyle routine, and within five hours it had had 200,000 views. Noble Warrior and Polly were going viral. Charlie warned him not to mention the Paralympic Podium Potential Programme. Polly didn't want to be subjected to unnecessary stress.

Noddy was enjoying a day off in the field with Percy.

Charlie watched them find the muddiest section. They pawed the ground with their hooves, churning up the earth and creating the perfect mud bath. Percy went first, folding down on to his knees and then rubbing himself all over. He rolled one way and then the other, covering himself so completely in mud that by the time he got up he looked bay rather than palomino.

Noble Warrior followed suit, flipping over three times before he clambered to his feet and shook himself. He snorted and stuck his tail in the air before galloping off at racing pace to the top of the field. Percy followed as fast as he could, looking furious that he had to make so much effort.

Charlie laughed and told herself it would all come off with a dandy brush, but she decided to keep them in the barn for the night so that they couldn't add to the mess they'd made. She and Polly watched the video Larry had taken of the National Championships, noting where the test could be improved and watching other riders for clues and tips on how to do it better.

'Do you know, watching the netball team and trying to work out where you guys can get sharper has really helped,' Polly said.

'How so?'

'It's made me much less self-conscious about criticism – I don't have to take it personally if a judge gives me four out of ten rather than eight out of ten for a move or even for my overall riding. It'll never be perfect because perfect just doesn't exist! Instead, I need to try and work out how to improve by tiny margins, every time I ride.'

Charlie pondered her friend's attitude and thought about the inspirational signs in the corridors at school. Polly might still be rebuilding her physical strength, but mentally – she was in a different league. It was impressive.

'Are you ready for the grand opening tomorrow morning?' Charlie asked. 'Your public will be out in force!'

'Ready as I'll ever be,' Polly replied. 'Have you

done your background check on the supermarket?'

'Yup,' said Charlie. 'I swear it's not like any shop I've ever been to. I reckon One Market could be a game changer.'

'You sound like a convert,' said Polly.

The next morning, Percy was woken up early and subjected to another sponge bath with bubbles. He was very grumpy indeed – two in three days was more than he could bear. Noble Warrior was far more gracious in his acceptance of the grooming.

Charlie and Polly had been sent sweatshirts in black and yellow with ONE MARKET written on the front. The boys had the same outfits with matching baseball caps. Charlie thought they looked like wannabe gangsta rappers.

Charlie was astounded to see how many people had turned up. The car park was rammed full and, as they turned the horsebox into its reserved space, she recognized several of the faces. Some of them had come to the Open Day at Folly Farm after Noble Warrior won the Derby. She also saw their headmistress, Mrs Kennedy, Dr Patterson and Mrs Wheeler who drove the school bus. Mrs Wheeler had brought her mother, who used a wheelchair.

'Is that Granny Pam's car?' Charlie asked her mum, pointing at a dark green convertible.

'She did say she might come,' Mrs Bass replied with a smile. 'You know she never likes to miss a showbiz event!'

As she climbed down from the lorry, Charlie heard her grandmother before she saw her.

'*Darlings!*' Granny Pam called out, running towards them with open arms. She was wearing a bright blue headscarf and glasses with matching blue rims. 'I'm so excited to see you! I've been reading that fabulous blog of yours and I am *so* proud to even know you!'

Granny Pam twirled Charlie round and then gently placed her hands on Polly's shoulders.

'As for you, my girl, I want to commend you for

that wonderful routine. I had to watch it four times just to be able to see it to the end through the tears.'

'No wonder it's had so many views,' said Charlie. 'Anyway, it doesn't take much to make you cry – I saw you sobbing over the theme music to *Emmerdale*!'

Granny Pam looked affronted. Hands on hips, she frowned at Charlie. 'How very dare you?' she said in mock outrage. 'That music is very moving. Thinking about it, I'm sure you could do a dressage routine to it. Maybe a medley of soap-opera theme tunes – *EastEnders*, *Holby City*, *Emmerdale* and Corrie. That would be wonderful . . .'

Charlie walked towards the back of the horsebox to lower the ramp.

'Great suggestion, Granny Pam. We'll certainly give it some thought.'

'*Doof, doof, doof* . . .' said Polly, mimicking the opening bars of the *EastEnders* theme. 'Could be quite dramatic.'

Charlie looked up and noticed that the

photographers had arrived. The local press were out in force and she recognized the man who took photos for the *Racing Post*. Harry must have been working hard to get all this publicity.

'Tell you what, Granny Pam,' she said. 'Could you do us a massive favour? Just go and talk to the press while we get ourselves together. That way they won't take photos before we're ready.'

'Me, talk to the press?' Granny Pam asked. 'But, of course. It's what I was born to do!'

She danced towards the gathering of journalists and snappers, her blue scarf fluttering round her neck. Charlie saw her pose for photos before engaging the press in conversation. She was good at this.

The car park was now so full that cars were backing up along the road and people were having to walk from further afield. Charlie noticed that One Market had three times as many accessible parking spaces as any supermarket she'd ever been to, and every single one was full.

She also saw a group of children and adults wearing Wilmington RDA sweatshirts. Miss Cameron was with them. Charlie and Polly waved and they all waved back.

'Hey, coach!' a voice called out.

Charlie and Polly turned round to see Flora Walsh and the netball team walking towards them.

'We brought someone who wants to meet you both.'

Charlie certainly recognized the woman who was with them. She had braided black hair with pink streaks in it. The woman reached out her hand.

'Pleased to meet you, Polly. And you must be Charlie?' she said.

Charlie nodded. She was speechless.

'I'm Ama Agbeze.'

'I know,' Charlie stammered. 'I know exactly who you are. You're the captain of the England Roses!'

'So pleased to meet you,' said Polly. 'I read all about your Commonwealth gold medal and how you developed the idea of *funetherness*. It's really helped us and that's how I'm going to get through this morning – by thinking of it as having fun together.'

'Good plan,' said Ama, raising her hand for a high five. 'Can't wait to see you do your thing and hear your speech!'

Polly looked at Charlie. 'What speech?' she asked.

Charlie looked around for her brothers and saw

Larry not far away. She shouted and beckoned him over. He was carrying two headsets and two small black boxes.

'These are your microphones,' he said. 'I've just got to fit them under your riding hats and put this on your waistbands.'

He pointed at the black boxes, which had metal clips on the back of them.

'Hang on a second.' Charlie cut him short. 'Why do we need microphones? You never said anything about giving a speech!'

'I didn't? Oh, sorry about that. Must've been a mix-up between me and Harry. We agreed that you and Polly should kind of explain, you know, what it's all about. It's not a speech as such – well, apart from the beginning bit where you have to welcome everyone and the end bit where you have to declare One Market officially open.'

Larry started fitting one of the black boxes to the back of Charlie's jodhpurs.

'Sort of thing you can do in your sleep,' he added.

Charlie didn't have time to be cross with him. She

was too busy thinking about what she wanted to say.

'We can do this,' Polly said. 'You're always saying that it's worth taking a risk for the things we care about and I think this is something worth caring about.'

Charlie nodded. Her mouth felt dry. At least Polly didn't seem nervous.

Once the microphones were fitted, they tacked up Noble Warrior and Percy, and got themselves mounted.

'You OK?' Charlie asked, patting her friend on the leg.

Polly beamed back at her. 'Hell, yeah! *Ama Agbeze knows who I am*. I've never been more OK.'

Charlie froze. Ama Agbeze was going to hear her speak. The captain of the England netball team, who was such a great speech-maker that she had the audience of *Sports Personality of the Year* eating out of her hand when they won Team of the Year. Ama had come all this way to see Polly, Noble Warrior – and Charlie. She had better make this good.

Charlie gave Percy a squeeze on his round tummy

and, together, she and Polly rode towards the entrance. Harry was talking to a smart-looking woman in a black suit with a crisp white shirt underneath. All the signs were in black and yellow to make them clearer to read, the doors were black with yellow edges and even the trolleys, were black with yellow handles. In fact, she saw a collection of powered trolleys, and low ones that had been adapted to use with a wheelchair.

The clock above the main entrance had black hands on a yellow background. It was five to eleven.

Larry appeared by her side.

'They'll switch your mics on at eleven on the dot and then it's over to you.'

Charlie looked down at him.

'Are none of the managers going to speak? Don't they want to introduce us or explain what the shop is about or what their opening hours will be? Don't they want to do some sales waffle?'

'No,' Larry replied. 'They're open twenty-four hours a day and they reckon that people will discover what they're all about by coming inside.

Mrs Patterson over there thinks it would be wrong to bore people with sales talk when they've come to see you and Polly.'

'Who's Mrs Patterson?'

'She's the managing director – and the sister-in-law of one of your teachers, apparently. Heard all about Polly way before she saw the blog. Funny old world, eh?'

Charlie looked at the clock. She had four and a half minutes to think of something to say. She patted Percy on the neck, hoping for inspiration. She saw Polly riding over to Mrs Patterson and watched them having a conversation. Charlie looked around the car park at all the people and noticed some fencing at the far end that looked as if it was protecting an open space. She wanted to know whether it tied in with the information she had read online. Harry ran over and handed her a leaflet which she scanned quickly, trying to take it all in.

At one minute to eleven, Polly rejoined her and, together, they looked around the crowd. As well as the Wilmington RDA group, she could see babies in prams, wheelchair users, people with guide dogs, people using mobility scooters, even a boy with Postman Pat painted on his prosthetic leg. She caught the eye of Nadia, who was standing with the netball team. Nadia gave her a thumbs up.

The clock started to chime behind her. Larry waved at Charlie as if he was a conductor cueing his orchestra.

'Testing, testing. One, two, three.' Charlie heard her voice echo out of the speakers that lined every section of the car park. She could also hear her voice coming out of the shop itself. She must be linked up to the speakers in there as well. The crowd fell silent and she saw hundreds of faces looking up at her expectantly.

'Welcome to the grand opening of One Market,' she began. 'My name is Charlie Bass. This is my best friend, Polly Williams, and we are proud to be here today, to sell you . . . an idea. She looked at Polly, who smiled and spoke confidently into the microphone.

'There are fourteen million people in this country who are disabled. I'm one of them, and all of us have to find solutions to everyday problems. How to get to work by bus if the one wheelchair space on that bus is already taken; how to navigate a building with a broken lift; what to do when there's only one accessible loo and it's out of order.

'If you have a mobility issue, every day is like riding in the Grand National with Becher's Brook or the Canal Turn standing in your way. I don't think that's right, and I am here to tell you that if we want the world to change, we have to find ordinary, everyday ways to change it.'

Charlie listened to Polly and wondered where she had found the confidence to speak so clearly and assertively. Polly looked at her and nodded, silently passing the baton. It was Charlie's turn to say something. She coughed loudly and heard the sound coming out of all the speakers.

'Sorry!' she shouted. Noble Warrior raised his head suddenly, startled by the sound. 'Sorry,' she said again, quietly. 'I'm not . . . I'm not used to this.'

Charlie's eyes widened and she swallowed. She knew she needed to get her thoughts together. Suddenly she remembered one of the books her mother had given her. She knew what to say.

'The Paralympics have shown us what elite athletes can achieve and they showcase the power of ability over disability, but not everyone can be, or wants to be, a Paralympian.'

Charlie saw Mrs Patterson nodding her head.

'You might want to be a musician or a doctor or a lawyer – but most of all, you want to be able to get into any building or on to any form of transport without a fuss.'

She paused. Granny Pam whooped.

'Sorry!' Charlie said. 'That's my grandmother. She's a bit overenthusiastic.'

She saw Polly's parents and her own parents standing together.

'Polly and I want to help change things for everyone. We want all of you to think about how *you* can make a difference. If we all work at improving the world around us, we will end up improving the *whole* world. One Market has created a shopping experience that doesn't use mountains of plastic, that gives you vegetables and fruit when they're in season – and they're going to use local produce, so if you want milk from cows that you can name, this is the place to come!'

She looked at her father, who shouted, 'Yay!' Charlie smiled and looked at Polly, who immediately took up the challenge.

'This is a place that is accessible and friendly and helps create a community,' Polly said. 'Mrs Patterson tells me there are going to be bingo nights in the café, book clubs, cookery classes, art classes. This is where you can make connections and care for each other.'

'And –' Charlie jumped in and pointed to a fenced-off area at the side of the car park where there were two all-weather courts and two pitches – 'out here there's basketball, seven-a-side football and netball.' She caught Flora's eye and grinned.

'This isn't just about turning up to buy things

you need and getting out as quickly as you can, or sitting at home clicking a button and waiting for it to be delivered. It's about making friends, sharing an experience, becoming part of a team, a family. Polly and I know, first hand, how good that feels.'

The netball team started clapping in appreciation and whooping their support. Ama Agbeze shouted out, '*Team up!*'

Polly took over. 'One Market is for all of us and, if there's anything you want to suggest to make it even better, just talk to any one of the OM team. They're in black and yellow so they're easy to spot.'

Charlie looked at Polly and mouthed, 'Ready?' Polly nodded at Larry and, as he hit the button, the heavy drumbeat started, together with the voices singing, 'Whoa, whoa, whoo-oh'.

Charlie raised her voice to say, 'Ladies and gents, this is the moment you've been waiting for . . .'

Polly joined in as they said together: 'We now declare One Market officially *open* for business. *Come on in!*'

Charlie and Polly turned Noble Warrior and Percy towards the doors, which opened automatically. The inside was dark, but as they entered, the lights came on. The floor was made of rubber, making it less likely that things would break if they were dropped, and making it less slippery for people (and horses).

The Greatest Showman was pumping out of the shop speakers. Noble Warrior and Percy started trotting in time with the beat, side by side down the aisle that said CEREALS AND BISCUITS. The lights came on as they went, turning right past the milk, butter and cheese.

'*Impossible comes true, it's taking over you!*' Charlie and Polly sang together. Polly asked Noble Warrior to go forward into extended trot. Percy's little legs went faster to keep up.

They trotted up every aisle until all the lights were on and the onlookers could see the goods on offer. As they came past the tills, the staff in black and yellow cheered.

Charlie stopped Percy by the fruit and veg

section to allow Polly to go forward with Noble Warrior into the open space where the daily offers would be stocked. Lots of people were crowding through the doors now and hundreds more were peering through the windows. As the music reached its crescendo Polly guided her horse to the star shape in the middle of the floor. Using this as her central point, she asked Noble Warrior to dance on the spot. She sat tall in the saddle and kept a strong contact with his mouth. She kept her leg firm and he started to trot on the spot.

'Piaffe!' said Miss Cameron to her pupils. 'Oh, that's very advanced.' They clapped in appreciation.

Charlie was captivated, but she still noticed Percy out of the corner of her eye, slyly stretching out to help himself to something from the shelf. Charlie laughed and tried to pull him away. Meanwhile, Polly was asking Noble Warrior to spin on his hind legs, turning on the spot to face the other way.

'Pirouette!' Miss Cameron clapped her hands together. 'Clever girl!'

'*It's everything you ever want, it's everything you ever need.*' The lyrics did the sales pitch for them.

'*This is the greatest show!*' Charlie and Polly sang at the top of their voices, before coming together and bowing to their audience. The applause rang loud and long before the crowds started their first shopping experience at One Market.

DANCING HORSE IS A ONE MARKET WINNER! read one headline the next morning. The papers were full of the story of Noble Warrior and Polly opening the new supermarket, and the film of them trotting through the aisles had made the news bulletins and got over a million downloads online. Charlie and Polly were looking at the papers over breakfast when the boys came charging into the kitchen.

'We've got bookings a go-go!' Harry told his sister excitedly. 'This is amazing.'

'The blog has got loads of new subscribers,' said Larry. 'What's more, we've had an email from the organizers of Olympia asking if we want a guest slot at the Christmas show and asking how much we would charge.'

'We've had a few enquiries about sponsoring the blog,' Harry added. 'One company asked if we would rename it *The Redline Racehorse Who Learned to Dance*.'

'What?' Polly asked.

'It's the name of a health company,' Harry explained. 'They insure people against illness.'

Charlie put her hand up to stop the rush of words tumbling from their mouths.

'Hang on. Hang on. This isn't what we did it for.' She looked at Polly as she spoke. 'We did this to give us a sense of purpose. We did it to give us something to aim for.'

'I thought we did it for the money,' said Larry matter-of-factly.

'Me too,' Harry agreed.

'No.' Charlie was firm. 'We did it to create a team and I think we've done that. We said yes to One Market because they're different. They believe in the same things we do – friendship, team spirit and celebrating difference. We're not going to say yes to every single offer just because it comes with a big fat pay cheque.'

'We're not?' Harry looked crestfallen.

Polly spoke up. 'I know you all did this for my benefit and I don't want to stop your business plans, but we need to have priorities, and Charlie and I have decided that training for the Paralympics is number one on the list. There's a Retraining of Racehorses class we can enter next month in Liverpool, and after that we need to be competing as regularly as we can.'

'Oh,' said Larry. 'So turning on the Christmas lights is out of the question?'

'It all depends where it is and what it's for,' Charlie reasoned. 'If we can raise money along the way for RDA, then it's always worth considering. After all, the team isn't just me and Polly. It's you guys as well.'

Harry and Larry puffed out their chests and fist-bumped each other.

'I guess it wouldn't have happened without you,'

Charlie continued. 'And I do realize that you were the ones who said Noddy had to pay his way. We can look at every request and discuss it as a team but I have one condition.'

'What?' asked Harry and Larry together.

Charlie picked up the newspaper and pointed at the photo.

'Next time they take a photo, you make sure Percy doesn't have a great big cauliflower sticking out of his mouth!'

QUIZ:
The Racehorse Who Learned to Dance

How closely were you paying attention when you were reading this book? Take our quiz to find out! But beware – the questions start off easy but get quite tricky at the end!

> TIP! Write your answers in pencil so the pen doesn't show through the page!

Q1. What is Noble Warrior's nickname?

....

Q2. Which three celebrities are the Bass cows named after?

....

Q3. How much prize money did Noble Warrior win at the Derby?

....

Q4. What kind of cake does Charlie's mum make?

....

Q5. Who suggests bottling a scent called Eau de Farmyard?

....

Q6. What is the name of the big horse race that takes place in Ireland?

....

Q7. What is the name of Harry's blog?

....

Q8. What kind of arena do Harry and Larry build for Polly and Charlie?

....

Q9. What is the term for when a horse stays in one spot and trots?

....

Q10. Who suggests using the word *diffability*?

....

Q11. Who is the captain of the school's first netball team?

....

Q12. Who suggests that Noble Warrior and Polly would be a good match?

....

Q13. What does Miss Cameron keep telling Polly to use to help her ride?

....

Q14. What startles Noble Warrior during his first visit to Wilmington RDA?

....

Q15. What position does Charlie play for her first netball game of the season?

....

Q16. What does Percy eat from the picnic basket?

....

Q17. Which movie do Harry and Larry use the songs from to make a medley for Polly's dressage debut?

....

Q18. What competition does Marjorie Pearson think Polly has the potential to compete in?

....

Q19. Who is Ama Agbeze?

....

Q20. What kind of company wants to sponsor the blog and suggesting renaming it *The Redline Racehorse Who Learned to Dance*?

....

Now check the next page to see how many you got right!

Answers!

Check your answers to the quiz below.
How did you do?

1. Noddy
2. Taylor Swift, Princess Anne & Madonna
3. A million pounds
4. Green pea cake
5. Mrs Williams
6. Irish champion stakes
7. *The Diary of an Ex-Racehorse*
8. A dressage arena
9. Piaffe
10. Charlie
11. Flora Walsh
12. Joe
13. Her *Buttdar*
14. His reflection
15. Wing defence
16. A cucumber sandwich
17. *The Greatest Showman*
18. The Paralympics
19. Captain of the England netball team
20. A health insurance company

15–20 correct:	Astounding! You are a true champion – first place!
10–14 correct:	Well done! You were just pipped to the post, but you're still in second place!
5–9 correct:	Not too bad. It's a third place rosette for you – better luck next time!
0–4 correct:	Oh dear. You may need to go back and read the story again to brush up on your know-how!

FIND OUT MORE ABOUT RDA...

RDA is a real charity – and there are hundreds of RDA groups just like the one that Polly belongs to.

RDA stands for 'Riding for the Disabled Association'

Let's find out more...

There are nearly 500 groups like Wilmington RDA all over the UK.

Altogether, RDA helps more than 25,000 children and adults just like Polly every year.

In the story, Polly competes at the RDA Nationals. This is a real competition!

The Nationals is the biggest event of its kind in the world for disabled horse riders and carriage drivers. Over 500 people compete every year.

HOW YOU CAN GET INVOLVED...

If you have a 'diffability', as Charlie would call it, and you'd like to try horse riding, why not ask your parents about contacting your local RDA group.

 Once you're 13 or over you can start volunteering with RDA. It's a great way to make new friends and spend time with horses.

All our groups need to fundraise so that more people can benefit. Why not organise a fundraiser for your local RDA group?

Horse riding really is good for you! Perhaps you could do a project for your school about how horses help people?

FIND OUT MORE AT WWW.RDA.ORG.UK

RDA It's what you can do that counts

Meet the Author

Puffin met up with author Clare Balding to ask her some nosy questions. Here's what she had to say …

Q. What gave you the inspiration to write about Charlie and Noddy, and how did you come up with the characters and their names?

A. I wanted a heroine at the centre of my story who was a bit different from everyone else at school and who had a great relationship with horses. I chose Charlie as her name because that's what I wanted to be called when I was young. I thought Noble Warrior was a rather fine name for a racehorse but all of them have a shorter nickname at home and I thought Noddy sounded better than Nobby.

Q. What advice would you give to someone who wants to be an author?

A. Make notes wherever you go – whether it's about people or events or places, notice the details and write them down. If you're planning a story, try to have an idea of where it's going before you start. Writing a bullet-point story arc or narrative outline is a good idea. Also, make sure you let things happen rather than just describe them as if it's an essay. My editor is always saying 'Show, don't tell'. Let all the senses come out in your writing – sight, sound, taste, smell and touch. Finally, don't be afraid to rewrite.

Q. What's your favourite sporting event to work at and why?

A. I don't present the horse racing any more but I do a lot of equestrian events like Badminton, Burghley and Olympia. I really love them. The riders are all really approachable and eloquent, so it makes my job much easier, and I love the whole atmosphere of equestrian sport.

Q. What's the funniest thing that's ever happened when you've been interviewing a rider (and their horse)?

A. Some horses are scared of the microphone because it's a big hairy thing, but some quite like the idea of trying to eat it, which has happened a few times and makes the interview sound extraordinary. I have a scene in my first book, *The Racehorse Who Wouldn't Gallop*, where Percy the pony tries to take a lump out of the microphone which is based on reality.

Q. What was your first pony called and what were they like?

A. My first pony was a Shetland called Valkyrie. She had belonged to the Queen who gave her to my parents for me to learn to ride on. She was small and round and furry and very particular about manners. My favourite pony was called Frank. I honestly think he was my first true love. I'm not sure he felt the same about me but I loved him all the more for his aloofness.

Q. Who is your biggest inspiration?

A. I'm inspired by all sorts of women who work hard and have achieved great things – Mary Berry, Helen Mirren, Judy Murray, Emma Thompson, J.K. Rowling, Billie-Jean King, Dina Asher-Smith, Lucy Bronze, Charlotte Dujardin, Piggy French. I could go on and on because there are so many great women who have achieved great things, but the most important thing is that you keep motivating yourself. As the German women's football team said in their World Cup video, 'When we need to see role models, we just look in the mirror'.

Q. What's it like being able to meet and interview some of the most famous riders in the world?

A. It's really wonderful and I never lose my wonder or forget how lucky I am. I got quite choked up when Piggy French won Badminton in 2019 because I've known her a long time and seen her just miss out on so many big occasions. She has gone through a lot, nearly gave up, and has driven herself back to the top of her sport. I am so impressed by the bravery and commitment of all those riders who keep at it for decades.

Q. Will you write another book about Charlie and Noddy?

A. I think *The Racehorse Who Learned to Dance* is probably the last in this series. It feels as if we've reached a natural end to their story. But I have lots more ideas for books, so watch this space . . .